THE MOUSE WATCH

THE MOUSE WATCH

J. J. GILBERT

Disney • HYPERION   LOS ANGELES   NEW YORK

Copyright © 2020 by Disney Enterprises, Inc.

All rights reserved. Published by Disney • Hyperion, an imprint of Buena Vista Books, Inc. No part of this book may be reproduced or transmitted in any form or by any means, electronic or mechanical, including photocopying, recording, or by any information storage and retrieval system, without written permission from the publisher. For information address Disney • Hyperion, 77 West 66th Street, New York, New York 10023.

Printed in the United States of America
First Hardcover Edition, November 2020
First Paperback Edition, July 2021
10 9 8 7 6 5 4 3 2
FAC-025438-21265
Printed in the United States of America

This book is set in 12-point Goudy Old Style/MT; Nexa Slab/Fontspring
Designed by Joann Hill and Sammy Yuen

Library of Congress Control Number for Hardcover Edition: 2019953767
ISBN 978-1-368-06820-8
Visit www.DisneyBooks.com

SUSTAINABLE
FORESTRY
INITIATIVE

Certified Sourcing

www.sfiprogram.org
SFI-01054

The SFI label applies to the text stock

For Emie

FOREWORD

When I was first informed of the incredible adventures that you're about to read, I could hardly believe my ears. I'd always heard rumors about the Mouse Watch, but I had no idea that the organization was still very much alive and in operation today until I spoke with Bernie Skampersky by accident. We ran into each other while she was on a rescue mission to save a cheese shop from burning down, and I can honestly say that it was one of the few tragedies that smelled as delicious as it was devastating for her entire village.

(That tantalizing scent of toasted cheese lasted for weeks, driving everyone in her village, Thousand Acorns, crazy with hunger.)

After Bernie obtained permission to speak with me from Gadget Hackwrench, her boss, the young agent and

I sat down for a series of long talks in which I learned, over many helpings of cheddar, Swiss, Brie, and bleu, about the heroic mice who work in secret to protect man- and mouse-kind every day.

It is my opinion that we should consider ourselves lucky to know, that while we sleep or go about our lives, blissfully unaware of the danger that might befall us, these tiny guardian angels are there to keep the world safe.

So it is my *enormouse* honor and privilege to chronicle some of the Mouse Watch's most famous cases and adventures that, until now, were kept TOP SECRET.

For the Watch!

—J. J. Gilbert

CHAPTER 1

Above the serene gaze of the most famous statue in New York, perched at one of the windows beneath her gigantic, seven-spiked crown, was an abomination.

The thing might have been a rodent once, but years of feeding the twisting rage in his belly had taken a toll on his outward appearance. He was now much more monster than mouse and more robot than rat. Besides his matted, gray fur, he also had metal hands and feet that clicked, clanked, whirred, and steamed with motorized rusted gears and spinning leather belts.

One of his eyes glinted with life but the other was dead glass. His entire appearance was the result of the cruel experiments once conducted upon him by humans.

Now, as he stood at the window, the thing's single-eyed gaze swept over the glittering lights of New York, taking in a stunning vista that stretched like a carpet of twinkling stars as far as the eye could see.

But Dr. Thornpaw didn't see beauty.

Beauty wasn't a part of his nature anymore. Pain and the temporary relief he felt when inflicting it on others was all he knew now.

When the doctor looked at the sprawling city, he saw only potential. Potential to fulfill the most evil and diabolical scheme he'd ever come up with. A true work of genius that would finally show man and beast what he was capable of.

It was something that the doctor felt would surely heal his pain.

As the last light of the setting sun faded into crimson twilight, Liberty's gleaming torch flared to life. For many, that eternally burning flame meant life and hope. But as the rays of golden light filled the crown room in which the rodent stood, the warm glow also illuminated a figure huddled in the corner and bound with ropes.

The victim was Ernie Mortenson, a human who had been, until a few minutes ago, a security guard at the Statue of Liberty National Monument.

He was supposed to retire next week.

But now he was Dr. Thornpaw's latest unwilling test subject.

Instead of hope, the light of Liberty's torch filled the

aging security guard with dread as it illuminated his monstrous captor, giving him his first clear glimpse of the thing that had imprisoned him. Ernie whimpered as several of Thornpaw's rat assistants leveled specially designed blowguns, each one poised to shoot a hollow dart that contained enough poison to fell thirty elephants. Ernie had always been told that rats were a problem in New York City, but he'd never expected to be attacked by ones that talked.

"Now, now, you mustn't struggle. Excess adrenaline might affect the results of my experiment and we wouldn't want that, would we?" croaked the doctor.

Ernie's eyes grew even wider as he gazed at the aggressive rat.

Thornpaw's feet clanked and hissed little jets of steam as he approached. Ernie wrinkled his nose at the scent of preserving chemicals and machine oil that surrounded the doctor. Although the human was far more massive than the doctor, the terrified expression on Ernie's face as he gazed down at the twisted rodent made Dr. Thornpaw feel like a titan.

After savoring the moment, the doctor glanced at the rat soldiers and nodded.

At the signal from their boss, the mob of rats encircled the whimpering man and, with surprising strength, hoisted him into the air. In seconds, they scuttled him down the spiral staircase to a waiting boat that was moored outside.

Dr. Thornpaw followed after, clanking and shuffling, whirring and clicking. He ran a long, ropy tongue eagerly over his sharp, yellowed teeth. The doctor was excited to begin the last test in a nearly completed plan. It had taken seventy-three other human subjects . . . seventy-three failures to perfect the formula . . . seventy-three negative studies that had resulted in all kinds of "interesting" reactions. Unfortunately, humans were resilient, and they'd fought back against all of his previous efforts to dominate their wills.

But the doctor had a very good feeling about number seventy-four.

Seventy-four would be the one.

CHAPTER 2

*D*on't look down!

It wasn't just the terrifying drop that bothered Bernie, it was also the fact that the plan she'd come up with to impress her idol, Gadget Hackwrench, wasn't being recorded by someone she trusted to do it right.

She glanced at her young helper and rolled her eyes.

Being the youngest child in a poor family meant that Bernie knew how to make the most out of a little. The young mouse had been born very sick, and although her health improved as she got older, she was still quite small for her age. It was a fact about herself that she hated, but had also learned to live with. And her helper was only a little smaller than she was, even though he was much younger.

Bernie was twelve.

Paul "Poopie" Longtail was only two years old, and Bernie knew that the little tyke wasn't supposed to be out at night with his babysitter having adventures. She watched as he tried valiantly to hold up a human-size smartphone with his baby-mouse arms, but he was clearly losing the battle.

It was also way past his bedtime.

"Hold it still, Poopie!" shouted Bernie. "Just get this one shot!"

"I . . . I'm twying," stuttered Poopie. "Thith themes weally dangerouth, Mith Bernadette. Maybe you thould get thome help!"

"No!" said Bernie. "I've got this. And please, Poopie, it's Bernie, not Bernadette."

"Thorry," said the baby mouse.

Bernie's long whiskers twitched in annoyance. She hated her full name. The only time she heard it was when her mother was upset and she was about to get in big trouble.

Bernie's tail was stiff and stuck straight out like a knitting needle, the usual sign that she was angry and about to lose her temper. Most of the time, when this happened, her family ran for cover.

But she wasn't angry.

She was scared.

The large paper clip she'd brought was attached to a fishing line that extended from the top of a rain gutter to a trash-can lid far below. She knew if she was going to try to get the attention of the most secret and elite mouse organization on the planet, she had to do something amazing . . . something that would set her apart from other recruits.

A warm wind ruffled her fur and rattled a set of wind chimes in the backyard below. Bernie breathed in the scent of dry earth and chaparral. It was a typical California night in September, but for her this night needed to be anything but that. It needed to be special.

Bernie thought of everything she'd tried so far to get the Mouse Watch's attention. She'd written letters. She'd created her own channel on MouseTube, the private, secure internet server created by, and for, mice. She'd posted several videos to the Underweb, a little known MouseTube channel that most fans believed the Mouse Watch organization secretly monitored. Bernie had tried doing crazy stunts, attempted to prove her intellect through solving puzzles, and had even resorted to begging in order for them to give her a chance.

So far, nothing had worked.

I've gotta make this one count, she thought.

She sighed, remembering all the bumps and bruises that she'd gotten along the way. Good thing "giving up" wasn't in her nature or she would have quit a long time ago. Coming into the world both sickly and small hadn't stopped her. Hadn't she'd surprised everyone, including her parents, with her courageous spirit?

But why hasn't it worked yet? Bernie wondered. *What's it gonna take to get Gadget to notice me?* She glanced down at the ground far below and suppressed a shudder. Would this finally be the thing that did it?

She thought of her older brother, Brody. He would have told her not to give up, and to never take no for an answer.

She missed him so much.

The wind picked up, slightly cooler now, cutting through the camo pants and black special ops sweater that Bernie always wore, a castoff from an old Commander Cody action doll. Her hair, dyed blue and worn high and stiff in the front, always looked windblown whether there was a breeze or not. It also added to her height, and the way she saw it, she could use any help she could get. Usually, the electric-blue color made her feel tough and daring. But the truth was, right now she didn't feel that way.

Bernie shivered, not from the cold, but from her nerves.

Then, steeling herself, she took a deep breath, adjusted her grip on the paper clip, and called down, "Are you recording?"

"Yesth!" Poopie lisped. "Ith been on for three minutes! Hurry, Misth Bernie! My armth hurt!"

It was time.

Bernie tried to calm her racing heart. Then, while

forcing herself not to think about how crazy she was being, she launched herself forward from the dizzying height and shouted,

"FOR THE WATCH!"

The speed was faster than anything she'd ever imagined. Every muscle in her arms ached as she held on for dear life. The wind howled in her ears and her whiskers were plastered to both sides of her cheeks as she rocketed toward the trash can below.

As she sped down the line, wobbling back and forth, she could see Poopie growing closer, the little tyke struggling to keep the phone from falling over as he recorded the stunt.

The glow of the screen came close.

For a nanosecond, she caught a glimpse of her own terrified but triumphant expression reflected back to her.

Then the fear faded away.

She was right on track.

Her plan was going to work!

All she had left to do was extend her feet and execute a perfect tumble, landing like an Olympic gymnast right in front of the smartphone.

But as it turned out, realizing that idea was much harder than it looked.

Later, when she recalled her inglorious landing, she remembered hearing two voices screaming in perfect pitch. Some part of her brain was amazed that she, a tweenage mouse, could make a screech that was as high-pitched as a toddler's.

She remembered a terrifying moment of slipping, sliding, banging, and shouting. Then, the world spun as she and Poopie went flying off the trash can into a thorny rose-bush. Miraculously, Poopie landed in the middle of a big rose, and the petals cushioned his fall.

Bernie wasn't so lucky.

Before everything went black, Bernie remembered hearing her leg crack when she hit the ground and feeling the agonizing pain that shot all the way up her back.

And when she woke up in the hospital, she found that her leg wasn't the only thing that had cracked. Her parents' smartphone, a rare, lucky find that they'd scrounged from inside an electronic recycling bin, had shattered on the sidewalk. The phone was the most expensive thing that her family possessed. It served as their wide-screen TV and internet connection to the larger world. It was also the only way Bernie could upload videos so that the Mouse Watch might find out that she existed.

Losing that phone effectively removed her very best (and most dangerous) attempt at impressing her hero, Gadget Hackwrench.

The Mouse Watch would never see the video.

And the hurt Bernie felt at that realization made her broken bone and her bruises pale in comparison.

CHAPTER 3

Bernie remembered the day that her life had changed forever.

It was a Saturday in July. Family day. The day that her parents made a point to connect with Bernie and her older brother. Brody loved it. They both did. Even though he was at that age where teenage mice usually didn't think it was cool to be hanging out with their parents and little sister, Brody was different. He loved family time.

And, even more importantly to Bernie, he loved spending time with her.

She adored him.

Bernie could still clearly picture the little gas station: FRANK'S BURGERS, GAS, AND SUNDRIES. The delicious smell of cooking hamburgers with bacon and sweet, homemade apple pie was hard to forget. It had been there since her parents were mouselings and even had its own ice-cream counter. The human owners had a soft spot for mice. And for as many Saturdays as Bernie could remember, they had set aside a tiny bit of vanilla ice cream and hot fudge on a plastic spoon in an overlooked corner of the shop for her family.

For Bernie's whole life, every Saturday had been the same. Sundae Saturdays.

Until it wasn't.

The white van marked MEDITECH LABORATORIES had seemed ordinary enough. It was parked in front of pump number nine when Bernie had arrived. Even now, her mind could picture it clearly because the painful day had been etched so permanently in her memory. Somewhere, back there, that Saturday played like a broken record, repeating the same tragic song over and over again.

It was Brody who had first noticed that something was off about the driver. Bernie had been so excited about the ice cream that she'd hardly been able to think about anything else. But Brody, who was a Mouse Scout, was always aware of the possibility of trouble. Always ready to help when others didn't notice or react.

Brody had noticed that the human's hairy arm was hanging out of the driver's-side window, listless and unmoving. The driver didn't budge when the pump stopped and the familiar electronic *ding* sounded to let the customer know that the tank was full. Minutes had passed.

Brody, in spite of his parents' warning not to get involved, had scampered to the van to see if anything was wrong. Like all mice, he knew the importance of keeping a low profile around humans. But Brody was a mouse built of high moral character. Even if the "rules" said to be careful, he was the first one to volunteer in a crisis.

Bernie had followed her older brother because she wanted to be just like him. Her parents had followed because they were worried.

Now, as she lay in her bed recovering from her bad fall, Bernie's eyes were closed tight. The memories seemed stronger and more vivid since her accident on the zip line, as if hitting her head had jarred them loose.

In her mind's eye she could see Brody, wearing his trademark mouse-size ball cap and hoodie. They were a birthday gift from their mom, two rare items from the Tony Falcon series of collectible skateboard dolls.

He'd been so proud of those clothes!

Bernie had watched, filled with admiration at her big brother's courage as he'd scampered to the van's window. As she drew closer, following in his footsteps, she saw the trickle of blood dripping down the driver's arm. Then, shortly after, she and her brother both saw the driver's pale, motionless face and his wide, staring eyes.

Bernie had been so mesmerized by the dead driver that she'd failed to notice the big warning signs displayed on a broken cage behind the driver's seat, signs that read DANGEROUS ANIMAL! and HANDLE WITH CAUTION! But Brody must have seen them. Some sixth sense must have told him that whatever creature had been locked inside was not only dangerous, but would have leaped at the first chance it had to escape and that it wouldn't have let anything, not a human driver and especially not a couple of young mice, stand in its way.

Brody, always alert, had assessed what was happening before his little sister had time to react to the sinister figure. Brody saw the glistening crimson stains on the escaped rat's mechanical claw and then dashed bravely in front of the open driver's-side window to block his path.

"Stay back, you!" Brody shouted. Bernie had automatically followed, standing next to her big brother, her eyes wide with terror. She hadn't been prepared for a confrontation with a dangerous rat and didn't know what to do, so she'd tried to imitate him and be brave, too.

Brody's warning had no effect on the rat. Bernie remembered how it sneered, baring sharklike rows of yellow, broken teeth. And then, to Bernie's horror, it had leaped directly at her with its claw outstretched, targeting the weaker of the two obstacles standing in its escape path.

"Bernie, look out!"

Brody, at the last possible moment, had pushed her out of the way as he leaped in front of the lab rat, receiving the blow from the creature's slashing, metal claw. The blow that was meant for Bernie.

To Bernie it had all happened in slow motion. She watched, horrified, as the mutated rat rushed by, emitting a raspy, jeering laugh that Bernie would never forget. There was the smell of chemicals, like the kind used to preserve the dead bugs they dissected in science class. Bernie had leaped out of the van window after him, screaming. It had been a bold move, one that she'd made without thinking. But she had been so blinded by pain and rage she hadn't given a second thought to any danger to herself.

Unfortunately, she was too late.

The one horrible swipe of that mechanical claw had ended Brody's young life.

Sobbing, Bernie had watched the rat run away and scuttle down a nearby sewer grate. The dangerous creature had escaped its cage, and she knew, with a strong sense of foreboding, that it would almost certainly do more evil things.

The anger and loss that Bernie felt that day had never gone away. In her mind's eye she could still see her brother's kind, smiling face and sparkling eyes. Just knowing that his furry face would never light up again made her heart ache with the deepest loss imaginable.

Brody had been the one who had always encouraged her. Brody had been the one who she could count on when she was at her lowest, assuring her that she was "small but mighty." Those words meant more to her than he would ever know. They meant that she was okay. More than okay.

That she was loved.

She'd vowed ever since that day to join the Mouse Watch and prevent such a thing from ever happening to others. She would follow in her brother Brody's courageous footsteps.

She wanted to make him proud.

***

"Please, Mom, no more soup!" Bernie cried. The terrible memories faded away as she stared at the spoon inching toward her face, filled with her mom's special recipe. "If I eat another noodle, I'm gonna barf!"

"You want that leg healed, you eat your soup," said her mother with mock sternness, pointing a doll-size ladle from the Chef Nancy set at the cast on Bernie's leg. Bernie grumbled and accepted the thimble filled with steaming broth and noodles.

Her mom's soup was delicious.

The lightly peppered mushroom broth was savory and spicy, and the homemade wheatgrass noodles were amazing. It had a wholesome, earthy smell to it with just a hint of lemon, and ordinarily Bernie would ask for a second helping. But at that moment, she was sick and tired of being cared for in bed. It made her feel like a baby.

"All right, then, how about dessert? Your father brought home a strawberry and we have some nice cake crumbs to go with it. What do you think?"

Bernie sighed and nodded. She didn't have the energy to argue. Besides, she never could resist dessert.

Bernie recalled the one time she'd found a half-eaten cupcake dropped by a human child outside a bakery. It had been, paws down, the best thing she'd ever tasted in her life. A sweet feast! But such lucky instances were very rare. The most a mouse could usually hope for was a crumb or two when foraging for human food. The good stuff was almost always snatched up by rats before the mice could get to it.

Thousand Acorns, the secret mouse village in which Bernie had been raised, had a little market, a tailor, a barbershop, three clothing stores, and a toy shop. The market was where all the mice did their shopping for groceries and household items, nearly all of them foraged from the human world and sold for prices that even the poorest mice could afford.

Most of the buildings had been constructed out of human things that had been thrown away. For example, the bank was made from a laundry detergent bottle, the tailor's shop was a shoe box, the clothing stores were built from coffee cans, and the toy store, Bernie's favorite place in the village, was housed inside what had once been a child's ukulele. The town was hidden inside a cluster of overgrown juniper bushes at the edge of a supermarket parking lot. They were quite prickly and mostly overlooked by the humans who hurried back and forth with bags of groceries. If the buildings were accidentally spotted between the branches, most people would have assumed that what they were seeing was simply discarded trash.

In reality, it was anything but.

The mice of Thousand Acorns had remodeled each of the shops with such artistry that they hardly resembled the trash they had once been. While the market where Bernie's mom did her grocery shopping still looked a lot like a broken dollhouse, all the damaged parts had been repaired, and inside it smelled of toasted sesame seeds, melted cheese, and fresh berries.

Bernie had been in bed for six weeks and was annoyed at being out of commission for so long. Since breaking her leg *and* her parents' phone, she was as close as she'd ever felt to giving up on her dream of becoming a Mouse Watch agent. Thankfully, Mr. Cheddarcheeks, the grocer, had kept her family supplied with all the wheatgrass noodles, broth, sweet cake crumbs, and cheese that they could ever need, things that he hoped would mean a speedy recovery.

Bernie felt a little guilty about what all these extravagances might be costing her parents, but was thankful that in Thousand Acorns, all the mice took care of one another. She knew that her parents would spend what little they had to nurse her back to health, and it warmed her heart to think about their generosity. She could imagine her brother's voice telling her not to be impatient or annoyed with her parents, that they loved her and were looking after her.

Instead of rolling her eyes, for Brody's sake, Bernie forced a smile at her mom and slurped up a noodle as noisily as she could. Her mom, doting as usual, dabbed her daughter's chin with a tiny square of napkin that she'd cut from a human-size Kleenex. The nice thing about being a mouse was that a single human-size thing could often be used multiple times in a tiny, rodent world. A single human Kleenex provided napkins for a month. And for a small mouse like Bernie, even a normal, mouse-size helping of anything was huge.

Bernie's mom was a stout mouse with brown fur and a trendy fashion sense. She worked as a tailor and ran one of the clothing shops in town. Most of the clothes were pilfered from human children's dolls and altered to fit a mouse's shape.

Bernie went to school at Acorn Academy, a cozy,

cylindrical building that had formerly been a large coffee can. Bernie loved the smell of coffee grounds and when she was lucky enough to have a donut crumb in her lunch bag, she thought that the delicious scent went especially well with the sugary snack.

At school, Bernie's favorite class was Mouse Tales, which covered the written history of prominent mice. She often wished she could do something noble and heroic enough to be written about in history books.

There was Martha Beadyeyes, one of Bernie's heroines, who'd led the great mouse liberation from the Cat King in 1776.

Then, in 1856, a group of three brothers, Ernst, Sven, and Gustav Von Scuttle, who were mountaineers, formed their own rescue team. They often went places that humans couldn't reach, and historical texts indicated that they rescued over one hundred avalanche victims in the Swiss Alps.

Bernie also admired Theodore Crumbsnack, a gentle and compassionate mouse who helped countless others escape from mousetraps during World War II. And she'd loved finding out that Winston Churchill kept a secret cadre of mice employed as code breakers. They were never officially listed in any historical texts, but a few photographs survived from that time, indicating that they were decorated as heroic agents by MI-6.

After school, Bernie would walk up the brightly

colored Lego stairs that led into her mom's shop and help her organize the inventory. Although she wasn't that interested in clothes herself, Bernie liked seeing her mom so excited whenever a new shipment of doll items was donated to the nearby human thrift store. The kindly human owner allowed her mother to have first dibs on the new stuff. In exchange, Bernie's mom helped the nearsighted old lady find small things she had dropped, like loose change and bobby pins.

After altering the doll-size clothes to fit a mouse-size shape, Bernie's mom would proudly arrange her creations on large, wooden clothespins that worked as mannequins so that all the mice in town could see them displayed for sale in the window.

Because of her mom's relationship with the thrift store, the majority of the furniture and decor in Bernie's house was thanks to the Summertime Nancy Home Collection. Bernie had to admit that having miniature items made a mouse's life much more comfortable than it would otherwise be. Of course, things like thimbles, matchboxes, bottle caps, and paper clips helped, too. Any of these things worked well for buckets, bowls, dressers, or washbasins.

Bernie's humble home sat on the edge of Thousand Acorns, near the thrift store, next to the supermarket.

She loved the fact that it had originally been built out of a human mailbox, something that—once it had been given walls and a smaller door—made for a perfect mouse house. Her father had found a half-full jar of paint meant for model airplanes and had used it to paint their home a cheery sunshine yellow. Their dining room table was crafted out of a small Tupperware lid, surrounded by four wine-cork chairs. Outside, the house even had a little mailbox of its own, which had been fashioned from a matchbox. It said SKAMPERSKY on the side.

It was very homey.

By tradition, most mice chose to imitate the big people's dwelling that they lived next to, and Bernie's house was no exception. The cheery yellow matched the trim on the human thrift store next to the supermarket. All mice were careful to keep their "version" of the human dwellings hidden from human view, for the first rule for all mice was to never, under any circumstances, draw any attention to themselves. The only humans to be trusted were ones that had been carefully studied for a long time to determine if they were "mouse friendly."

If an unkind human decided to set traps, call an exterminator, or, worst of all, get a cat, the results could be cat-astrophic.

There was nothing scarier than a cat.

That's why the entire village was surrounded by an alarm system called "Fee-lines." It was a weblike system of strings and alarm bells designed to detect a cat's crossing. If a feline crossed a Fee-line, the "fee" the cat would pay would be an entire village of angry mice armed to the teeth with air horns and spray bottles, two things guaranteed to make any cat think twice about attacking.

Bernie had heard that other mice weren't so lucky. For example, the surfer mice who lived in Malibu had to rely on a lifeguard watch that stayed on guard all night. If a cat was spotted, all the mice took tiny surfboards and escaped to the waves, a chilly prospect if one was caught in the middle of sleep. The best, most coveted surfboards were small plastic key chains pilfered from the souvenir shops that lined the boardwalk. Less fortunate mice relied on flimsy body boards made of old tongue depressors or wooden spoons.

Malibu mice had to be especially careful, since cats that roamed the beach were feral. The cats of Thousand Acorns were mostly house cats that had escaped through screen doors left ajar.

If the rumors Bernie had heard were true, the celebrity mice who lived among actors and actresses in the Hollywood Hills made a point to form solid relationships with the numerous pampered pooches of the Hollywood elite. Dogs were more curious about mice than they were aggressive toward them. In general, they were much more open-minded animals. If you made friends with one, Bernie had heard, they would give you rides on their furry backs and fend off hungry cats.

Having a dog as an ally went a long way.

"Bernie . . . BERNIE!"

Bernie heard her dad, Clarence, call in his baritone voice. It was a voice that sounded tired from a long day's work. It was also a voice that always had an edge of anxiety in it, a voice that was constantly worried that something terrible might happen to Bernie. She had noticed that change in both of her parents after Brody's death. It seemed like she could hardly do anything since that tragic day without them checking in on her, making sure that she was safe and that she wasn't getting into any trouble. She couldn't really blame them, but sometimes it felt suffocating.

Bernie's dad was an accountant. He liked to wear large black-rimmed glasses, gently used bow ties, and secondhand tweed vests. He was also, as he proudly put it, "married to the best-dressed mouse in the community," even though everyone knew that they were also the poorest.

"Still in bed, Dad. Haven't moved," Bernie called back. Then she added, muttering to herself, "Pretty hard to go anywhere with a broken leg."

Clarence opened her bedroom door and glanced at his daughter over the top of his spectacles. He looked worried.

"Did you sign up for a credit card again?" he asked.

"What? Me? NO!" she replied, flustered. She'd hoped he'd forgotten the time when she'd tried posing as a human adult, sneaking into the local library after hours and using one of their computers to apply for a charge card with a fifty-thousand-dollar limit. She'd wanted to buy an online series of rock-climbing videos because she knew that an agent should be able to handle even the most difficult situations. She'd also wanted to have the extra credit in case she needed to buy her own one one-hundredth scale electric toy motorcycle, a dream she'd had for several years now. The thought of zipping around the streets looking to rescue people in danger was a thrilling concept.

The application hadn't worked. And worse still, her dad had freaked out when they'd gotten the rejection letter and found out what she'd been up to.

"Well, that's good," her dad said with a relieved sigh. Then he handed her a large, bulky envelope. "Looks like something came for you."

Bernie never got mail. Feeling uncertain, she accepted the package. It was indeed addressed to her. But when she looked for a return address, she was surprised to see that nothing was written there.

"Huh," she said. Then, after a shrug, she tore open the mouse-size envelope.

Her eyes widened.

Her whiskers twitched.

And her heart leaped so high within her chest, she thought it might have flown straight up and out of her mouth.

There, lying on her crisp white bedsheet, was a glittering golden gear about the size of her paw.

It can't be, she thought. *There's no possible way.*

But there it was, and it could only mean one thing.

It was the legendary Mouse Watch recruitment invitation. Something she'd dreamed about. Something she'd hoped to one day hold in her hand. But something that deep down she didn't believe she would ever see. Conspiracy theorists on MouseTube didn't even believe it existed. There were whispers, sure. But nobody she knew in real life or followed online had ever seen one.

Until now.

And the thing . . . the really amazing thing about it, which left no doubt as to where it had come from, was that there was an iconic signature etched onto the gear. She knew that signature. It was signed at the bottom of every poster plastered on her bedroom walls. The signature of her hero.

Gadget Hackwrench.

The famous mouse inventor had sent this to her personally!

Even though Bernie hadn't uploaded the video of her amazing zip-line act of courage, the Mouse Watch had still, somehow, found her.

Could they have made a mistake?

Bernie's mind raced. She thought about the other videos she'd uploaded. None of those seemed impressive enough. Why her? What had she done to be considered for this honor?

She quickly dismissed the thought. At that moment, she was too excited to care.

Her parents stood, gazing at her with confused expressions.

"What's that?" asked her mom, pointing at the glittering invitation.

"Are you building something? If you needed a gear, I'm sure I could have found one for you at a discount," her dad said. The apprehension in his voice told Bernie that he assumed she'd ordered it online. "That looks expensive," he added.

"I didn't buy it, Dad. Don't worry," Bernie said. Then she rubbed an anxious paw up through her tall, blue bangs, stiffening them even higher than they already were.

"Um, Dad, Mom, can I please have a little privacy?" Bernie clasped her paws in a begging gesture. "I . . . I just need some time to myself."

Clarence and Beatrice glanced at each other with confused expressions, shrugged, and then left the room, closing the door quietly behind them. Bernie wished she could share this moment with Brody. He would understand what a big deal it was.

She turned the gear over and over in her hands, examining it closely. At first, she didn't see anything besides Gadget's autograph. But then, after staring so hard her eyes began to hurt, she noticed a tiny row of letters and numbers etched faintly on each of the gear's teeth.

"It's a test! A puzzle," she whispered excitedly. Then she added, in a barely audible whisper, "I love puzzles."

Which was, technically, an understatement. Bernie *lived* for puzzles.

She studied the etchings on each tooth of the gear— an arrow followed by a sequence of random numbers:

10 7 26 16 22 4 2 15 19 6 2 5 21 9 10 20 19 6 17 16 19 21 21 16 22 15 10 16 15 20 21 2 21 10 16 15 16 15 16 4 21 16 3 6 19 20 6 23 6 15 21 9 2 21 20 6 23 6 15

"Hmm," said Bernie with a smile. "This looks fun. . . . "

Everyone knew that Bernie wasn't much of an athlete. As evidenced by her zip-line fiasco, most of her attempts at ninja acrobatics had also failed miserably.

And she also wasn't much of an inventor like her heroine, Gadget.

But when it came to numbers, Bernie had inherited

both her dad's love of equations and her mother's artistic creativity. The combination was rare and also very potent. She was one of those few individuals for whom numbers and art were virtually inseparable.

As long as she could remember, Bernie had visualized numbers as if they were imaginary friends. In her mind, each one had a different personality. For example, when she pictured the number twelve—her favorite number—she saw a stick of peppermint candy standing next to a twisting blue worm she'd named Freddie. When she was little, she made up all kinds of stories about Freddie and the letters he would write to the Candy King, hoping to be invited to the Sugar Castle. The castle was made of candy, and the candy was shaped like numbers, too.

Math was a creative, fun place to play.

Her incredible brain was equally split between logic and art, and that made her one of the greatest puzzle-solving geniuses that had ever been born.

At least, Bernie thought so. And she hoped that the Mouse Watch did, too. Maybe *that* was why she'd been chosen.

Inside her brain, a rainbow cornucopia of shapes and symbols, numbers and letters superimposed themselves on top of each other as she considered all the possible solutions to the code. Her mind swirled with brilliant colors, abstract shapes, and beautiful number combinations. The integers were spinning like bright pinwheels and whispering solutions in her mind as she sorted and carefully filed them into hidden mental compartments. This was the fun part.

After a few minutes of sorting through numbers and making connections, she took a final glance at the golden invitation and noticed something unusual, something she hadn't seen at first.

Her grin widened.

"Gadget, you're brilliant!" she shouted. "Why didn't I see it before?"

She glanced up at the posters of Gadget that lined her walls. They were the size of human postage stamps (actually, they *were* postage stamps) and most of them had inspirational sayings written on the bottom:

DON'T GET MOUSE-TRAPPED BY MEDIOCRITY! GIVE 100%!

BEING SMART ISN'T CHEESE-Y! STAY IN SCHOOL!

But all of them had one thing in common: Gadget's autograph.

Gadget had an unusual, one-of-a-kind signature that was famous for being hard to read. Up until that moment, Bernie had believed that it was just the inventor's quirk— even geniuses could have bad handwriting.

But now she realized nothing could be further from the truth. She gazed down at the signature on the gear.

As she stared, the letters morphed into colorful numbers in her mind.

The "G" in Gadget was really a number "8."

The "A" was a "2."

The "D" was a "5."

The next "G" was also an "8."

The "E" was a "6."

The "T," of course, was a "7."

Feeling confident, Bernie plugged the numbers into the code—but the result was still gibberish!

Then, before her eyes, the bottom part of the 7 morphed into something she recognized: Freddie, the blue 2! It wasn't a 7 at all, but actually two numbers on top of each other: a "2" and a "1."

The "T" was a "21."

And that's when her whiskers twitched in triumph.

She had it.

She had the key to the code.

She felt it in her bones before she even plugged in the numbers. That feeling of knowing—that was the *best* part.

The first code Bernie ever learned was a basic "substitution code": A=1, B=2, C=3, and so on. The first letters corresponded with their matching number.

Easy peasy.

When she first saw the numbers etched into the gear, her instinct was to substitute them with their corresponding letters to spell out some kind of message. But all she came up with were nonsense words.

However, when she realized that the letters in Gadget's magical signature were really numbers, everything became clear. Gadget's name was actually telling her which letters corresponded with which numbers in the substitution code! G was the seventh letter in the alphabet, but in Gadget's signature, it was actually, literally, an 8. That meant if you plugged it into the substitution code, G was one number off from its order in the alphabet. The A in Gadget's name was a 2, which meant that the substitution code would start with 2 instead of 1. Then B would be 3, C would be 4, and so on.

In other words, the alphabet would look like this:

A=2 B=3 C=4 D=5 E=6 F=7 G=8 H=9 I=10 J=11 K=12 L=13 M=14 N=15 O=16 P=17 Q=18 R=19 S=20 T=21 U=22 V=23 W=24 X=25 Y=26 Z=1

The solution was both simple and complex at the same time. Most people would have wasted a long time trying to figure out why the numbers didn't line up.

Bernie's whiskers twitched with pride.

After she looked at the numbers etched on the gear again, the message quickly became clear.

This: 10 7 26 16 22 4 2 15 19 6 2 5 21 9 10 20 19 6 17 16 19 21 21 16 22 15 10 16 15 20 21 2 21 10 16 15 16 15 16 4 21 16 3 6 19 20 6 23 6 15 21 9 2 21 20 6 23 6 15

Became this: IF YOU CAN READ THIS REPORT TO UNION STATION ON OCTOBER SEVENTH AT SEVEN.

"October seventh!" Bernie exclaimed. She glanced at the calendar on her wall. It was the size of a human credit card and had the words *Farm and County Insurance* printed at the top.

October seventh is tomorrow!

"Mom, Dad! Come here, quick!" Bernie shouted.

After a scuffling noise in the other room, her harried-looking parents appeared at the door. "What is it? What's wrong?"

Bernie held up the gear and, smiling broadly, announced: "You'll never believe it," she said. Then, after pausing to let the enormity of the incredible news have its full impact, she gazed at their expectant faces with sparkling eyes and added, "I've been recruited for the Mouse Watch!"

CHAPTER 4

"Um . . . the What-watch?" asked Bernie's mom, looking puzzled.

"The Mouse Watch! The most secret, cool, impressive group of mice ever assembled!" She leveled a stare at her parents. "I need to be at Union Station tomorrow! I've gotta pack!"

They stared back, dumbfounded.

"Pack?" her father said. "For what?"

"Wait. You guys really haven't been listening to me, have you? I've been talking about the Mouse Watch since I was six," Bernie said.

"I . . . I thought it was some kind of alarm clock," admitted her dad with a shrug.

"I thought it was a game you made up," said her mom. "And you have a broken leg," she added.

"It's totally healed by now! See?" She hobbled around

the room, trying to show that she could put weight on her leg without squeaking in pain. Her mom crossed her arms and looked unconvinced. So Bernie grabbed the nearest thing she saw, a doll-size plastic wrench on her matchbox nightstand, and tried to pry the cast from her tiny leg. "I'm fine, Mom, really. Watch!"

"Stop!" shouted her mom, panicking. "Just . . . stop! You might still be healing! Dr. Finetail should decide if your cast is ready to come off or not."

Bernie didn't look up. She just kept prying away at her cast.

"Bernie," her mom said.

Slivers began to make their way down the plaster.

"BERNIE!"

Craaaaack.

"BERNADETTE APRIL SKAMPERSKY!"

Bernie finally looked up at the sound of her full name. Her mother never yelled like that.

"Mom, please, I don't have time! I have to be there at seven in the morning!"

Of course, Bernie realized, the message hadn't said whether she was supposed to be at Union Station at seven o'clock in the morning or at night. Getting there early seemed like the safest bet.

"We don't know anything about this Mouse Watch," Bernie's father said.

"Where is it?" added her mother. "Who will you be staying with? How do we reach you?"

"What will you be doing?" her father asked. "More stunts like the one that broke your leg?"

"I'll be saving the world!" Bernie cried. "Haven't you heard of the Rescue Rangers?"

Her parents stared at her with confused expressions.

"Okay, so they used to be this really famous detective agency started by these two chipmunks named Chip and Dale, right?" Bernie grew excited, gesturing wildly as she described her heroes. "And they had this incredible female mouse on the team named Gadget Hackwrench, who was, like, their inventor and mechanic. Gadget left to start her own spin-off group—it's basically like the MI-6 of mice! It's this small group of elite agents who travel the world solving crimes using mouse-size tech that Gadget invents herself! And best of all, they're not in it for the glory. They're in it to be heroes! To totally help anyone in need! And I'm going to be one of them!"

Her parents shared a look.

"You're not doing this, Bernie," said her father quietly.

"What?" squeaked Bernie, aghast.

"What your father is trying to say," said Bernie's mom, sharing her husband's worried glance, "is you've been acting very irresponsibly lately, and we think it's time for you to settle down. You're twelve now. You have to start thinking responsibly."

"I do think responsibly!" Bernie retorted. Her tail was stiff as a board and her whiskers were twitching with emotion.

"But you don't," said her father sternly. He pointed at her leg. "That isn't thinking responsibly. And what about before that, when we caught you taunting the human neighbor's cat with a laser pointer?"

"I was testing my reflexes! Every Mouse Watch agent has to have lightning-fast reflexes!" Bernie argued.

"Wearing a laser pointer tied to your own tail and trying to get an animal ten times your size to chase you is not okay. You could have been killed!"

"The Big World is dangerous for such a small mouse," her mother said. "There are bigger threats out there than house cats."

"I know," Bernie said, her voice cracking. Angry tears were welling in her eyes. "That's why the Mouse Watch needs me!"

How could this be happening? Why couldn't her parents understand? This was the most important moment in her whole life, the thing she'd wanted for as long as she could remember.

And all they could see was how much of a failure she was.

"Bernie," her dad said, "all we've tried to do, ever since . . ." He paused and started again. "All we've ever tried to do is protect you, so you can have a good life. Isn't there anything else you want to do, anything that's closer to home? Something fit for a mouse?"

"We think you should focus more on other things," Beatrice said gently. "Like making friends. We never see you doing things with anybody your own age. Maybe you could—"

"Don't you think I've tried?" interrupted Bernie. "I'm not like them. I don't even understand what half of them are talking about! All they care about is whose parents have pilfered the newest smartphone, or the latest Summertime Nancy collection. I don't care about that stuff!"

"And just what, may I ask, is wrong with clothes?" asked Beatrice, bristling. "It might do you good to wear something other than those . . . those . . . army things. You might even feel better about yourself." She brightened with an idea. "You know, I've got a new pair of pink plastic pumps that would be adorable if you'd just let me—"

"NO!" shouted Bernie. "That stuff is good for *you*, Mom, but it's not me! How many times do I have to say it?"

"Watch your tone, young lady," said Clarence sternly. "Your mother is just trying to help."

"Sorry," Bernie mumbled. A tear slipped down her furry cheek and caught in her whiskers.

Her dad's expression softened. He could see how upset his daughter was.

"You're really good with numbers," he said. "How about coming to work with me? Maybe I can get you an internship? How does that sound? I could train you to be an accountant."

Bernie sniffed and swiped at her pink nose. "Dad, thanks, but I don't want to be an accountant. Being part of the Mouse Watch is all I've ever wanted. Ever. And if I don't do this now, I'll have missed my chance forever. They don't ask you twice. I'll never be able to . . . to . . ."

She didn't finish her sentence. But it seemed, from their somber expressions, that her parents knew what she'd been about to say. They knew that she wanted to honor Brody's memory by dedicating her life to helping others. For Bernie, it meant that all the things Brody stood for still mattered. That her brother hadn't died in vain.

Bernie stared down at the golden gear, hating the sight of her sad reflection in the shiny surface. This was supposed to be the happiest day of her life. She'd never been so close to her dream, and now it was slipping away.

Clarence and Beatrice stared at each other for a long moment, each reading the other's thoughts. Finally, Clarence cleared his throat.

"You'll call as soon as you get there?"

"And give us this Gadget Hackwrench's *direct* phone number?" her mother said sternly.

"And take your vitamins every day."

"And absolutely no stunts!"

Bernie's heart swelled.

"Yes! I'll e-mail you every day! And I won't do any-thing reckless. And I'll get stronger, I promise!"

Her father sighed.

"I'll go contact Dr. Finetail."

As her dad left the room, her mother moved to the side of the bed. She laid a gentle paw on her daughter's shoulder and sighed.

"Let's get you packed. If we're going to get you to the train station, we have to leave now. It'll take hours for us to get there in the Jeep."

Bernie didn't know what to say. All she could do was throw her arms around her mother and squeeze as tightly as she could.

CHAPTER 5

The Moorpark train station was, according to the internet, twenty minutes away from Thousand Acorns by gas-powered human car. By remote control toy Jeep, however, it took several hours. Not only did mouse drivers have to be on the constant lookout for speeding full-size human cars, but they also had to be on special guard against other predators. Hawks and vultures that flew along the highway were always hungry, and legend had it that monstrous beasts called raccoons lived in the brush that lined the roads. Bernie had never seen one, but a mouse in her class swore he spotted one near the dumpster outside the supermarket.

And you always had to look where you were going, or else you would end up as something horrifyingly called "roadkill," which was exactly what it sounded like, her mother told her with wide eyes.

As a precaution, Clarence had consulted the tiny map at the back of their wall calendar to find as many back roads as possible. Now, as they bounced along in the plastic Jeep, Clarence had both paws gripping the remote control in the front seat while also peering into the gathering darkness and watching carefully for any dangerous obstacles. Since the toy Jeep had stickers where headlights should be, Beatrice held up a small flashlight that had once hung from a human key chain to illuminate the road ahead.

Tonight, the air smelled of eucalyptus and dry grass. In October, the California weather could be unpredictable, alternating between warm Santa Ana breezes and cold days that hinted at the winter to come.

Bernie loved autumn and would usually have paid more attention to a nighttime drive filled with seasonal smells and long moonlit shadows. But her mind was elsewhere at the moment.

She absently felt up and down her leg through the outside of her camo pants. It felt strange to have her cast gone after wearing it for so many weeks. Luckily, Dr. Finetail had been available at such short notice. So far, it seemed that there were so many ways her once-in-a-lifetime opportunity could have gone wrong. Even now, as they rumbled along in the toy car, listening to the battery-driven whine as it bumped down the side of the road, she hoped nothing would interrupt her destined meeting with the Watch.

"Dad?"

"Hmm?" replied Clarence, deep in concentration.

"You checked the batteries right? Are they fresh?" asked Bernie worriedly.

"Yep. And I put an extra four-pack of double As in the trunk. Stop worrying."

But it was impossible not to. Bernie kept running the decoded message over and over in her mind. She had to be there by seven in the morning. Had to. Everything had to go just right.

In the backseat, she stared over the top of the doll-size suitcase her mom had lent her. It was part of a vintage Flight Attendant Nancy ensemble from the 1990s and was a bright, glittery pink. Her mom had bestowed it on her as if it were the holy grail of luggage, beaming with pride.

"It's a collectible," she'd said proudly.

Bernie hadn't wanted to hurt her feelings, so she accepted it with a forced smile. She glanced at the empty spot in the backseat next to her and wished, for the millionth time, that her brother was sitting with her. She could imagine him rolling his eyes at the sparkly suitcase, understanding completely what she was feeling.

Bernie examined the round suitcase with its glittery, bright pink plastic surface complete with a rainbow cloud sticker and winced. It really didn't look like secret-agent material, and she hoped that she wouldn't be laughed at by the other recruits.

I wonder if there ARE other recruits? Bernie thought. *Maybe I'm the only one. Maybe I'll get special, one-on-one training from Gadget herself.*

There were so many questions she had no answers for. She couldn't help the steady stream of "what-if"s that trickled through her mind like a leaky faucet. For the first time in a long time she was filled with hope. She felt convinced that the mice of the Mouse Watch would be like her. It would be, finally, a place where she would be understood.

Where she would belong.

It had to be.

Nowhere else seemed to fit.

Because of careful planning (and more than a little luck), Clarence pulled into the ramshackle Moorpark train station at three a.m. The toy Jeep was black and blended in nicely with the shadows, ensuring that it could stay well hidden. As she climbed out of the backseat, Bernie glanced at the familiar sticker license plate that read JUNGLE J. The remote-controlled Jeep was part of the line of Jungle Jay action-figure accessories. Her mom had created Bernie's military-style outfits from those toys, which was a challenge because of the bulky action figures they'd been originally created for.

The toy Jeep was her father's pride and joy and he loved

it about as much as her mother loved her Summertime Nancy collectibles. Unfortunately, Bernie's cool, "special ops" image was compromised a little because of the silly suitcase her mom had given her. The closer she got to her arrival at the Mouse Watch, the more self-conscious Bernie was starting to feel about her appearance. She desperately hoped that they wouldn't underestimate her based on her tiny size. And it really didn't help her feel more confident when she pulled her glittery suitcase out of the backseat of the car. Why had her mom made her take that one? Wasn't there anything less conspicuous?

Most places in the human world had a corresponding mouse-size counterpart if one knew where to look. At the Moorpark train station, Bernie and her parents knew that the small ticket office was carefully tucked away behind a potted plant. It was made from a child's sand bucket and was painted red with brown trim. It also had the same old-fashioned shingled roof as its counterpart. As Bernie and her family drew close to it, she noticed that sitting behind the ticket window was a very nice-looking old mouse. He wore a dark blue conductor's cap on his head and had an impressive droopy, white-whiskered mustache.

He was also snoring.

"Er, excuse me? We're looking to go to Union Station in Los Angeles," said Clarence.

The old man snorted, startled, and then adjusted his bifocals to peer at his customers.

"Whoops! Dozed off there. Tends to happen this time of night," he said with a yawn. He glanced at his pocket watch. "Whoa! You're a bit late for the midnight special, but we got the red-eye heading out in, oh . . . 'bout ten minutes. Tickets for three?"

Clarence and Beatrice exchanged nervous glances.

"Um, how much are the tickets, exactly?" asked Bernie's mom.

"Let's see here," said the old mouse, consulting a notebook. "Union Station. Round trip is twenty-three dollars per person."

"Twenty-three? Is that in human or rodent currency?" asked Beatrice worriedly. Rodent currency was smaller than human currency and was sometimes exchanged at different rates.

"Same for both," said the conductor.

Bernie nervously bit her nail as she watched her parents whisper. Clarence checked his wallet, and Beatrice riffled through her purse. Both were shaking their heads, a bad sign.

No, no, no, thought Bernie worriedly. *Please no. We're so close!*

Suddenly she remembered that she had a little money in her pocket. She pulled out a five-dollar bill with the image of Theodore McFurry, the first president of the Mice of the United States.

"I can help!" she said excitedly, stuffing the bill into her dad's paw.

Clarence looked at it and sighed. After glancing at his wife, he handed the crumpled bill back to his daughter, gently closing her fingers around the money.

"You might need that," he said quietly.

Bernie overheard her mom whispering with the conductor. Moments later she returned and handed Bernie a gleaming white ticket.

"We only had enough for one, sweetheart," she said.

Bernie stared at the white slip of paper that represented all of her hopes and dreams. She glanced back up at her parents, who stared back at her with worried smiles.

"If you don't want to go alone—"

"No . . . no, I'll be fine," interrupted Bernie. "I . . . can do this."

They stared at each other for a long moment.

"Mom, Dad, I can't thank you en—"

But she was drowned out by the lonely, echoing blast of a diesel horn. Bernie glanced down the tracks and saw a pair of bright lights coming toward them.

The rest of the good-bye went so fast. There were tight hugs. There were also a few tears.

And the next thing Bernie knew, she was aboard the

gigantic train. Her heart pounded as the mouse conductor escorted her to a small row of seats that had been built beneath the human-size ones. There was only one other mouse traveling on the red-eye to Union Station, fast asleep in the window seat.

The engine started.

The wheels started slowly turning.

Then, as the train pulled away from the station, Bernie was able, for the first time, to let out a sigh of relief. She was actually going. Nothing had stopped her.

Union Station, here I come!

And whether it was from all the excitement or because it was the first time she'd been able to slow down since they'd left the house, Bernie felt her eyelids grow heavy.

I'm doing it, Brody. Just like you said I could.

As the human conductor made his way through the car, taking tickets from the human passengers, the mouse conductor scurried down Bernie's row, taking tickets from the mouse passengers hidden in the shadows beneath the human seats. Bernie could hardly keep her eyes open. After handing the conductor her ticket and getting it stamped, she fell asleep before the caboose had pulled past the Moorpark ticket office.

She was soon dreaming of becoming the best Mouse Watch agent that the world had ever seen.

CHAPTER 6

The first thing that Bernie realized when she disembarked at Los Angeles Union Station, was that she needed to get out of the way of the stampede of wing tips, loafers, tennis shoes and high heels that threatened to squash her underfoot. She dashed as quickly and calmly as she could. Her parents had taught her that anytime she was in the presence of humans, she should avoid scampering. The big people had an uncanny knack for noticing things scuttling near their feet, and it was dangerous for a mouse if spotted. Bernie had heard tales of high-pitched screams and pest exterminators being called, just because a mouse had scampered accidentally.

Bernie moved stealthily and deliberately, making her way in the shadows to a large trash can where she could hide, unobserved.

From her vantage point, the view was limited. But she saw the big clock in the station and it read 6:50 a.m.

"Well, at least I'm on time," she murmured. Her stomach rumbled, and she realized that she'd forgotten to pack anything to eat. Bernie tilted her nose into the air and sniffed, trying to determine if there was any hope of finding some nearby crumbs.

The station smelled of highly polished wood, age, and the slight diesel-y odor of train engines. But, thankfully, there was also the scent of bacon and eggs coming from a quaint-looking food stand in a corner of the waiting area.

Bernie's big brown eyes scanned the distance between the trash can where she was hiding and the restaurant. She could see a few of the patrons eating stacks of syrup-drenched pancakes and breakfast sandwiches. Her eyes narrowed, focusing in on a five-year-old human girl eating a donut. Little humans were well loved by mice because they almost always dropped some of whatever they were eating.

Bernie's mouth watered.

"Why do there have to be so many big people around at this time of the morning?" she mumbled. The direct route to the food stand had heavy foot traffic, and there didn't seem to be many places to sneak that wouldn't be out in the open. It was a bad idea to attempt a food grab.

Bernie sighed and pressed her tiny paw to her rumbling tummy.

What now? she wondered. *Will somebody come and find me? Where am I supposed to go?*

She reminded herself not to panic. She was the farthest she'd ever been from home, and scary, nervous thoughts were trying to push their way to the front of her mind. One thing that Bernie was usually good at was being brave. It wasn't that she didn't feel scared sometimes. Everyone did. But Bernie was unique in that she never let panicky thoughts keep her from doing what needed to be done.

However, she'd also never quite done anything as daring as riding a train all the way to Los Angeles by herself before, and she felt just a little bit wobbly in her knees.

Bernie bit her thumb nervously as she watched the minute hand on the big clock finally tick to twelve.

There was no accompanying chime or bell.

Nobody in the station paid it a second thought.

But Bernie's keen eyes spotted something. A tiny, furry face peered out from behind the number six on the clock, opening it like a door, and it scanned the crowds with a miniature pair of binoculars.

A Watcher! Bernie thought excitedly. She decided to pull a risky move and emerge from her hiding spot so that the mouse could see her.

Bernie was so excited that she didn't take stock of her surroundings before darting out and waving her paws at the mouse high up on the station wall. And her impulsive decision came with a price.

Grrrooooowwl.

Bernie stopped waving. A sudden icy chill raced down her spine. Glancing over her shoulder, she saw a *terror*!

Technically speaking, it was called a "terrier." But this one was definitely a terror. Whereas most dogs were curious, friendly beasts, she could see by the look in this one's eyes that it didn't like mice.

Not one bit.

From Bernie's small vantage point, it was huge. Its giant black eyes were riveted upon her, and the hackles on its neck bristled like a cactus.

"Juno, shhh," said Juno's owner, an old woman who was oblivious to what her dog had seen. Bernie knew she only had a split second before total chaos erupted.

"Nice doggy," Bernie whispered.

The dog wasn't stupid. It knew the difference between a human command and a little mouse trying to act like it was in charge.

"ROW! RAWR! RAWR! RAWR!" The little dog burst into a series of aggressive barks. With a bound, it leaped from the lady's lap and raced toward Bernie.

"Juno! Come back here!" shouted the woman.

Bernie saw a massive white muzzle with giant pointy teeth racing straight at her.

It was a choice between flight or fight. Most people, if faced with a dangerous furry monster, would have probably run as fast as they could. But Bernie had been practicing ways to face danger for several years now, ever since the first videos she'd uploaded to try to impress the Mouse Watch.

Instead of running, she planted her feet and raised herself as tall as she possibly could. She stared at the oncoming beast with steely resolve in her eyes and, as it drew close, she yelled in the loudest voice a small mouse could muster, "STOP!"

Juno the terrier wasn't at all prepared for such a booming command to come from such a small creature. With a loud whimper, the dog scuttled back on its hind legs and then, yelping loudly, rushed to the safety and security of its owner's lap.

Bernie's heart was beating fast. It had been a frightening moment. But her triumph was short-lived when she realized that in the commotion she'd broken the rule observed by intelligent mice everywhere and especially by the Mouse Watch.

A mouse must NEVER draw attention to herself.

And Bernie's shrill cry of "STOP!" had, indeed, drawn

the attention of the entire train station. Everyone in the waiting area froze, staring down at the tiny talking mouse wearing Jungle Jay action-figure clothes, with various expressions of amazement.

Bernie felt the towering crowd inch closer. This time, there wasn't an easy path for escape. Legs like massive tree trunks surrounded her, and there wasn't even a gap of daylight to slip through. Then she heard the shrieks and squeals that were always followed by pest control.

Oh no, what have I done?

She thought back to all the warnings her parents had given her as a child, telling her that the delicate relationship between humans and mice depended on the mice never being spotted. Her dad had taught her all about the dangers of mousetraps. He'd even shown her one once, and the loud snap it made had given her nightmares for weeks.

She knew also that some humans could be trusted, and there were stories of the big people being kind to mice. But even so, allowing them to know that you could speak their language was strictly forbidden by the laws of nature. It was illegal. It just wasn't done.

And now, she'd done it.

A humming noise came from somewhere above her, growing louder by the second.

Bernie glanced up and saw a gleaming white drone zip into view, hovering on four whirring propellers high above the crowd of people. A voice she recognized boomed from a speaker, a voice that belonged to the mouse she admired most in the world.

"Humans of Union Station, if I could have your attention." Mercifully, the crowd's attention was diverted from Bernie as they looked around to see where the mysterious voice was coming from. "Yes, you. All of you. Look up here, please."

A hundred faces turned to look at the drone.

"Thank you!" The voice echoed across the station. "And now . . . good night!"

Tiny jets of purple mist shot out of the side of the drone. Bernie thought it was one of the most unusual shades of lavender that she'd ever seen. It seemed to sparkle and glow with particular intensity. Then, as the mist cloud settled over the upturned faces, the crowd of eyes glazed over, and almost as a unit, the entire human population in the station began to yawn.

Bernie stared, amazed, as one by one all the people in Union Station decided to lie down and take a nap. If they were already sitting, they started snoring where they sat. If they were standing, they knelt down and curled up right there on the floor.

Then, as the purple mist finally made its way down to the floor, Bernie felt her own eyes grow sleepy. The room was starting to spin.

Two long cables fell from the drone, followed by two mice rappelling down like expert mountain climbers. As Bernie's eyes began to flutter closed, she noticed that the mice were dressed in jet-black jumpsuits with silver piping and were wearing glowing blue goggles. They also wore portable oxygen masks, and she felt one being slipped over her nose and mouth just as she began going under.

Seconds later, with cool, pure oxygen filling her lungs, Bernie felt the effects of the gas fade away. The oxygen she was breathing seemed to carry with it some kind of antidote to the sleeping mist because Bernie noticed it also smelled and tasted kind of minty.

"Bernie Skampersky?"

But Bernie was so overwhelmed, she couldn't even remember her name. She just stared openmouthed at the two Mouse Watch agents, then back up to the hovering drone, so overcome that she couldn't speak.

Finally, after a long moment, she managed to squeak beneath her mask, "Is Gadget inside there?"

The agents chuckled.

"No. It's a recording," the first agent said in a clipped British accent. Bernie noticed that her fur was a tawny brown and her brightly dyed red hair was clipped into a sharp bob just below her chin. The second agent looked much older, and he had a military-style buzz cut. He indicated the sleeping humans and added, "The Sleep Spray is her invention, though. When these folks wake up, they won't remember a thing."

He turned his attention back to Bernie. "You ready for a ride?"

Bernie nodded excitedly. The red-haired mouse spoke into a walkie-talkie on her shoulder. "Leo, we have the recruit. Returning to base." Then she added, with a nod and a wink at Bernie's glittery suitcase, "Nice luggage."

And as Bernie was hooked into a harness and raised up on a cable into the gleaming white drone, she felt like she was dreaming.

It had finally happened.

She was on her way to the Mouse Watch headquarters.

CHAPTER 7

SHOOOM, ZRWOOOW, SHUSHHHH!

The drone swooped and dipped, narrowly missing a flock of pigeons that had flown into the station. Bernie held on with white knuckles, trying desperately to hang on to the last meal she'd eaten (when had that been?) as the drone looped and sped at breakneck speed through the train station and hurtled toward a crack in an open window high up near the vaulted ceiling.

As the drone sped closer, Bernie was just able to make out the tiny opening. They were going to fit through *that*? It looked way too small for the drone, and Bernie's heart leaped into her throat as they drew closer . . . closer . . . CLOSER!

"Aaaaaahhhhh!" In spite of her trying to hold it in, a scream ripped out of Bernie's throat as the drone suddenly tilted sideways, navigating the narrow space with a whisker's length to spare.

"Ha! Made it again!" shouted the red-haired mouse. "Way to go, Leo!" Bernie, who was still shaking, noticed that she directed this comment toward the cockpit of the drone.

"That was quite a stunt you pulled back there," said the red-haired mouse, removing her goggles and glancing at Bernie.

Seeing her face for the first time, Bernie noticed she had big blue eyes and long eyelashes. She also looked to be about Bernie's age, which made Bernie's heart sink. She remembered all the times she'd tried to make friends with the mice in her class and had failed miserably.

"Um, thanks, I guess," Bernie replied awkwardly as she removed the oxygen mask from her face. She wasn't sure if the mouse was giving her a compliment or not.

"Standing up to a Jack Russell," said the burly, military-looking mouse. He shook his head and chuckled. "That really took guts!"

"Hey . . . you hungry?" said the redhead, turning her attention to a small pack at her waist. She pulled out a plastic pouch with two large peanuts, a raisin, and a big piece of yellow-coated chocolate candy.

"We have some trail mix. There's better food back at the base, of course, but if you need a snack . . ."

Bernie was starving but she was also feeling self-conscious. She waved off the gesture, saying, "No thank you." But then her stomach rumbled loudly. Bernie blushed furiously. "Okay," she said, "I guess I *am* kind of hungry."

The red-haired mouse laughed good-naturedly and handed Bernie a salty peanut and the yellow-coated candy drop. Bernie took a big bite of the candy. Her parents never let her eat dessert first, but they weren't here. As she munched, the redhead grinned. "My name's Alpheba. Everyone calls me Alph," the mouse said, extending a paw.

Bernie shook it, and forcing herself to overcome her trepidation about mice her age, managed a smile.

"Hi, Alph."

Bernie looked around at the cabin of the high-tech drone. "This . . . is amazing," she said.

Alph nodded. "Yeah, Gadget designed a whole fleet of them. They're mainly for crowd control like you saw back there, helping people forget that they've seen us so that we remain secret. So far, knock on wood, we've only crashed one. Ninety-nine trouble-free missions."

Before Bernie had time to ask about the one that went wrong, the other mouse extended his paw. As Bernie shook it, she noticed he was missing his little finger.

"Craddock McMuenster, but you can call me Digit."

He released her paw and wiggled the missing bit where his finger used to be. "Lost it to a R.A.T.S. operative. HA!" he chortled. He glanced at Bernie, seeming to size her up.

"You might be the smallest recruit I've seen. What

happened, forget to eat your spinach?" he said with a wink.

Bernie's expression must have shown that size was a sensitive topic, because Digit immediately held up his hand in apology. "Don't misunderstand! If there's one thing I've come to realize in my vast years of experience at the Watch it's to never underestimate a recruit based on appearance. Why, I remember one guy, what was that mouse's name?" He snapped his fingers, remembering. "Charlie Twitchynose. Tall and skinny as a beanpole. But I saw him personally take out three R.A.T.S. operatives using nothing but a strand of spaghetti and a stick of gum. Don't ask me how he did it, I wouldn't be able to tell you."

Bernie chuckled. She couldn't say why, but she liked Digit right away. She could tell he really hadn't meant anything by observing how small she was. After all, most people reacted with surprise when they saw her. But the fact that he seemed so accepting of her appearance made her feel that he was okay, a nice older dude who didn't judge anybody.

Glancing down, Bernie noticed that Digit carried some cool-looking gadgets on his belt. She pointed to an odd-shaped hook in a holster and couldn't help asking, "Wow. What's that?"

"This?" said Digit, glancing down. "It's a zip-line grappling hook. Designed it myself. It actually saved my life during that skirmish I mentioned. You should have seen what happened to the other guy; I gave him something to remember *me* by." His expression changed, his eyes gazing out into some imaginary time and place.

"I was twenty-three. Still a new recruit. First mission turned out to be Moscow. 'Bring it on,' I said. Nothing I couldn't face. I was king of the world. After a chase through St. Petersburg, there we were, me and a rat three times my size, squaring off on top of a fountain. I had never learned how to swim, never saw the need for it. But you'd better believe right then I wish I had! I knew it was him or me. I reached for my handy zip-line grappling hook and—"

"Pleeaaaase, Didg . . . let's not tell that story again, shall we? I really don't want to talk about R.A.T.S. right now." Alph rolled her eyes. "She just got here. There's plenty of time to catch her up on all your adventures. She probably has a dozen questions."

"Rats?" asked Bernie.

"R.A.T.S.," said Alph, spelling out the letters. "It stands for Rogue Animal Thieves Society. And, yeah, they're mostly rats, too. A few other creatures here and there. A snake. Some mean iguanas."

As Digit rattled off the other creepy species of Rogue Animal Thieves, Bernie shivered as she remembered the one time she'd encountered a rat.

The horrible creature that attacked Brody had almost certainly been a rat at one point, before it had been fused with metal appendages. She could tell by the long, thick tail, and bloodred eyes. She would never forget those eyes. They made her fur stand on end. Ever since that day, rats were her biggest fear. She believed they were always lurking in the shadows, waiting for a chance to strike.

"I actually have a lot of other questions. . . ." said Bernie, making a list in her head. She was just about to ask one of the thousands of things that she'd wondered about the Mouse Watch when a voice from the drone cockpit interrupted her.

"Save it, rookie! We're approaching HQ. Radio silence and buckle up."

"Roger that, Leo," said Alph. She leaned over to Bernie and whispered, "Better do as the pilot says. All your questions will be answered at orientation later."

Bernie found the seat straps, and after fastening the shoulder belt, she suddenly felt the drone lurch forward with an unexpected blast of speed.

"HQ, this is Pepperjack Alpha, we're coming in," Leo's voice crackled over the radio.

After a moment, a second voice crackled back, "Roger that, Pepperjack, you're clear to approach."

The overhead lights inside the drone's cabin snapped off. Dimly lit, blue LED strips that lined the floors and windows flickered on, casting a ghoulish aspect on the passengers. Bernie held tight to her armrests and gazed outside the tiny windows as the drone continued to pick up speed. Bernie could see the Union Station's iconic outdoor clock tower, located just off the main terminal building, growing closer.

Slow down, she thought. As before, this pilot seemed to like pushing for some kind of speed record as he navigated small spaces. But unlike before, as the clock face grew closer she couldn't see anyplace for the drone to land. It looked like they were going to crash directly into it!

At the last possible moment, a narrow door, precisely the width of the drone itself, slid open inside one of ten decorative alcoves above the clock. The drone shot inside, a lightning-fast maneuver obviously designed to attract as little attention as possible.

Bernie had always imagined riding in a drone. But after this short trip she decided drones were definitely overrated. At least motorcycles had their wheels on the ground.

Once the drone was inside, the door slipped closed just as soon as the back rotors cleared it. Bernie gulped as the entire view outside the windows plunged into total blackness, and she wondered where she was and exactly what kind of dangerous training she'd gotten herself into.

CHAPTER 8

Two bright spotlights appeared on either side of the drone, emerging from a shaft in the darkness somewhere far below. Bernie stared out the window as the aircraft began to descend like an elevator.

There was really nothing to see out the window but the dark walls of the inside of the clock tower. The drone steadily descended . . . and descended . . . and descended until Bernie realized they must have already reached the bottom of the tower and were now continuing underground.

Minutes passed.

Bernie couldn't help feeling a bit claustrophobic as she thought of the hundreds of feet of rock that must be overhead. She was just about to ask how much farther it would be, when she felt a slight bump.

The hum of the propellers stopped.

Then a doorway slid open, and bright blue light streamed

into the cabin. Bernie had been in the darkness so long that it felt like she was looking directly into the sun. She blinked, and after her eyes adjusted, she followed Digit and Alph out of the cabin and stared around in amazement.

She'd always wondered what the Mouse Watch's head-quarters looked like, often imagining something right out of a spy movie.

But nothing, NOTHING, could have prepared her for the incredible high-tech chamber that greeted her.

She'd never seen anything like it!

Bernie felt a paw on her shoulder and turned to see Alph grinning at her. "This is my favorite part of welcoming new recruits," she said, gesturing before them. "Welcome to Mouse Watch HQ."

Bernie gaped.

She gasped.

Her whiskers twitched and a huge smile stretched from ear to ear.

The room was the size of a human airport terminal. The mammoth space was gleaming white, with glowing blue lines traversing the walls. The first things she noticed were the massive, transparent tubes that crisscrossed the length and breadth of the building. She was amazed to see grinning mice shooting back and forth inside them, buoyed by what seemed to be vacuum air currents that plastered their fur and whiskers flat to their faces.

"Zoom Chutes," said Alph, noticing Bernie's stare. "They get you where you're going as quickly as possible. We don't like wasting time here at the Watch."

Below the Zoom Chutes, on the floor of the main terminal, Bernie noticed Watchers scampering everywhere, some talking into white, wireless earbuds, which must have been communication devices. There was a low hum of chattering voices, police scanners, and, to Bernie's delight, the whirring of robotic vehicles.

Some looked like saucer-shaped Roomba vacuums that had been souped up with newer, more powerful motors and a small seat for a Mouse Watch agent to ride on top. Each one was piloted by an agent in an orange jumpsuit and a sleek helmet, and they glided expertly around the room, narrowly avoiding each other and the many pedestrian agents.

Around the perimeter of the cavernous room, big glass cubes with glowing edges divided up the space, creating little offices or work spaces. Bernie noticed that many of the glass walls had semitransparent images projected onto them, displaying websites or digital maps. Some mice were using them as touch screens, pulling up surveillance cameras and database information with the swipe of a paw.

Bernie sniffed happily. The place smelled clean and fresh, with just a hint of lemon disinfectant cleaner. The room was bustling in its own well-organized chaos; a group of highly trained agents operating with clockwork precision and timing.

Like a watch.

The agents all wore jumpsuits in different colors. Many of them wore the same black jumpsuit with silver piping that Alph and Digit were wearing. The pilots wore orange. Others wore crimson, and only a few were dressed in gold. Each one sported at least one badge on the front, and some agents had many. Bernie didn't know if they were to indicate rank, or to show some kind of achievement or award, but the different decorative touches looked impressive. When she was little, she'd wanted to join Mouse Scouts but her overprotective parents never let her. She'd loved the idea of getting badges and awards for her accomplishments even then.

I want one of those uniforms so bad! she thought. She dreamed of one day covering it with badges.

She wanted to ask Alph and Digit what the colors of the jumpsuits and badges meant, but decided instead to save her questions.

Slow down, Bernie. You'll get a chance later, she instructed herself. *Right now, you need to just observe. Take in all you can. Who knows? There might be a test later.*

She decided to trust her eyes and ears. She'd often

found that by watching and listening (and sometimes smelling), she could find answers to questions before she'd even asked them.

She stared with awe as her eyes followed the agents. She couldn't believe she would soon be one of them. *Gadget is just one mouse, but she started all of this. Wow. What a genius!* Bernie thought.

She was so eager to get started training it made her stomach hurt.

Digit rubbed his big paws together and grinned. "Okay, rookie, time to get the nickel tour. You ready?"

"Totally!" Bernie said, nodding happily.

Alph put her paw on Bernie's shoulder and motioned broadly, encompassing the entirety of the large hangarlike building that they were standing in.

"As I said before, this is HQ," Alph began. "It's the nerve center of the Watch. This is where agents from all over the world check in after a mission for debriefing." She smiled. "Think of it as the battery."

Digit motioned with a tilt of his head to a nearby glass cubicle where an agent in a black uniform held her paw next to a palm reader. "Post Operation Processing. POP for short. After each mission the agent's identity is verified. You'd be surprised at some of the sneaky tactics we've seen over the years. Enemy operatives trying to pass themselves off as Watchers."

He barked a laugh. "HA! Most of them have no idea what they're in for. Gadget's tech is so good, it would take a genius to sneak past our haptic readers and DNA tests. Impossible, really," he said.

"Okay, let's go this way," said Alph, motioning for Bernie and Digit to follow. Bernie would have liked to stay longer to watch the entire process of the agent getting checked in after her mission. She longed to hear what kind of adventures she had experienced out in the field!

She might have saved a world leader or stopped an invasion of some kind. Man, I wish I could pick her brain. She glanced around the incredible, high-tech facility as she followed Alph and Digit to a set of double doors.

As she took it all in, Bernie realized something: Everything in the building had been specifically designed by—and for—mice. There wasn't a single item from the Springtime Nancy Collection or Jungle Jay. No doll furniture here! No human-designed plastic toys or bottle caps, either. How someone had designed tiny versions of the most cutting-edge tech she'd ever seen was beyond her understanding. It seemed impossible! And yet, all the mice were using the tech without a second thought, as if it were the most normal thing in the world.

In fact, the only examples of human-size objects in the building were things that the Mouse Watch seemed to be using for training purposes or for analyzing clues.

Bernie caught sight of a human-size pencil in one of the glass-enclosed offices, the teeth marks indented upon it being analyzed by a mouse in a lab coat making notes with a stylus on a mouse-size tablet.

Brody would have loved this.

She realized it with a twinge of both sadness and happiness. Her brother was crazy about technology. He was the one who had shown Bernie how to access the internet via her parents' smartphone and who had proudly given her the secret password for the Mouseweb when she'd turned six. She remembered how he'd put his arm around her shoulder and tousled her hair, telling her that she was big enough to use it. *Big* enough. He always used words that made her feel tall and important.

Bernie's thoughts were interrupted when the three of them placed their security badges in a scanner, and Alph and Digit led her through the doors into a darkened chamber. It took a minute for Bernie's eyes to adjust to the darkness. She heard Digit's voice from somewhere just ahead of her say, "Get ready, rook. What you're about to see is gonna blow your mind!"

"No need to be so dramatic, Didg," said Alph's voice. "It's cheesy."

"Ummmm, cheesy," said Digit. Bernie could hear smacking sounds as he licked his lips. "I could go for a big plate of melted Gorgonzola right now."

Bernie snickered. But her giggle turned to a gasp when she heard a switch flick, and shafts of glowing blue light suddenly illuminated several glass-enclosed training stations. The interior of each one was vast, all containing a variety of themed training exercises for Mouse Watch agents.

"Careful, you'll catch a fly with your mouth hanging open like that." Digit chuckled. Bernie, who had been staring slack-jawed at the glowing training rooms, snapped her mouth shut.

"Hey, we're in luck. Here come some agents. Now pay attention, you might learn something," said Alph.

Two gruff-looking male Watchers with a tough-looking female between them entered the first training center. All three wore the same glowing blue goggles that Digit and Alph wore. Bernie watched as the three nodded to each other and then pressed a small fingerprint sensor on the side of his or her goggles.

The three gigantic holographic rats that appeared in front of them looked so startlingly real that Bernie jumped. Each one had a weapon at the ready and began firing as soon as it materialized.

The three agents leaped and twirled to escape the rounds of laser fire, hitting back at the holo-targets with expert marksmanship. To Bernie it was like watching a deadly, acrobatic circus performance. The agents moved with expertly timed martial arts prowess, but even with their obvious skill, a couple of them got blasted by the holo-rat agents. When one of the virtual laser blasts hit an area on a Mouse Watch agent, a light flashed on their haptic suit, logging the hit.

A giant scoreboard was projected on one of the glass walls, keeping track of the hits for each team. Bernie was swept up in the exciting spectacle and cheered for her favorite agent, the wiry female who ended up being the last mouse standing.

When the drill was completed, the blue floodlights that illuminated the practice room turned red and each of the agents removed their goggles. As they compared scores, Digit turned to Bernie and said, "The program can be adjusted according to the skill level of the agent. That's a little string of code I added, with Gadget's permission, of course."

"It looks like fun," said Bernie. "How soon can I try it?"

"Ha! Not so fast," said Alph. "You've got to pass basic training before you get to do these tests." She grinned at Bernie's eager expression and then added with a wink, "But with your spirit, I'll bet you'll be here in no time at all."

Bernie glowed from the praise.

Digit led the way to the next room, in which there were already a dozen or so agents in workout gear running through an obstacle course filled with trampolines, monkey bars, tackling dummies, and tumbling mats.

"Daily workout," said Digit. "An agent has to remain in top physical condition." Bernie suppressed a giggle when she saw Digit sucking in his potbelly as he spoke. Alph snorted and said, "The only time I've seen you run is when they're serving cheese crumpets at breakfast."

"Nonsense!" said Digit, pretending to be affronted. "I run at lunch and dinner, too. You never know if they might be serving mac and cheese."

All three laughed. Bernie found that she really liked her new friends. She couldn't remember the last time she'd shared a laugh with anyone.

The last time was probably with Brody, she thought. Ever since his death she'd felt the weight of the world on her tiny shoulders. But right now, even though she missed him terribly, she was feeling good—better than she had in ages!

The last room in line was empty save for a single figure standing inside it. Digit ran his paw over the scanner and they went inside. As they moved closer, Bernie saw that the figure was actually a mouse made entirely of white plastic and chrome, with glowing blue trim. Its eyes shone as its head swiveled around, surveying all three of them.

"This is a Candroid," said Alph.

"You mean android?" asked Bernie.

"Nope, I mean Candroid," said Alph, smiling. "As in the droid 'Can' answer almost anything you ask it. I know the name is kind of cheesy. But Gadget came up with it, so it stuck."

"I voted for naming it Ann," said Digit confidentially. "Ann-droid seems a lot friendlier than Can-droid."

Alph turned to the robot mouse and asked, "When do Mouse Watch agents stay indoors?"

The machine didn't even pause before answering, "When it's raining cats and dogs."

"Ha!" Digit laughed.

"I don't get it," admitted Bernie.

"It's not very good," said Alph. "Jokes really aren't its specialty. Try asking it something hard."

Bernie thought for a moment. "How many R.A.T.S. operatives are there in the world?"

The machine didn't hesitate before answering, "One million three hundred thousand four hundred and six. Not including the one currently on the premises."

"Currently on the premises? That can't be right," said Alph.

"Must be a glitch," added Digit. "I'll have my guys in tech support run a diagnostic later today."

"We don't currently have any R.A.T.S. operatives here at the base," Alph explained to Bernie. "Sometimes we bring them here for processing before they head to trial, but as far as I know, we haven't conducted any raids today."

"Got one coming up on Tuesday, though," added Digit. The big mouse glanced at his watch. "We'd better get a move on. Orientation is about to start. But before we do . . ."

His voice trailed off as he approached a large metal cabinet mounted on a nearby wall. After swiping his iden-tity card, he opened the door. Bernie's eyes lit up when she saw an array of high-tech goggles lined up inside.

Digit removed a pair and with a big grin tossed them to Bernie.

"Didg . . . I don't know if we should yet," cau-tioned Alph.

"It's under my purview," said Digit. "As tech officer I get to decide when and where a recruit gets a pair of goggles. Right here is where, and when is now. Try 'em on, Bern!" he said with a grin.

Bernie couldn't believe it. "Do you mean . . . these . . . are mine?" she asked hesitantly.

"Yep! Your first piece of agent gear. Those goggles are some of the best tech we have here in the Watch. I like you, kid. You remind me of myself when I was your age, except that I was, well, quite a bit larger."

Grinning widely, Bernie slipped the goggles on her head

and placed the lenses over her eyes. She'd seen pictures of Gadget with her goggles countless times and had always wondered if there was more to them than met the eye.

Sure enough, there was.

Seeing the world through the glowing blue lenses was like looking into a secret dimension. Special markings became visible on Alph's and Digit's uniforms, denoting secret ranks and achievements. Little floating tags appeared next to them, indicating information about who they were, their standing heart rate, their individual likes and dis-likes. A tag next to Digit read, *Likes: Cheese of all kinds. Dislikes: Cats.*

The blue-lit, glass-enclosed rooms that she'd seen earlier were filled with digital markings and secret technology centers. She could see a virtual computer bay next to the Candroid and various notes that were invisible to anyone not wearing goggles. As she gazed at them closer, they seemed to be notes about locations of various R.A.T.S. bases.

"This. Is. Amazing," said Bernie, enunciating each word as she stared around herself with awe.

"They can do tons of things. There's a virtual owner's manual in your room," said Digit, obviously enjoying the young recruit's reaction.

"Didg, we really gotta go," said Alph worriedly. "She'll be late and you know how Gadget feels about punctuality."

As she trotted after the agents, Bernie tried not to stare

around at all the amazing readouts she could suddenly see, for instance, the glowing blue line beneath her feet that showed the way. The tag next to it said "To Orientation" and had a countdown clock next to it.

Tiny words flashed in the bottom left corner of her goggles: Covert Status: Neutral.

"Hey, wait up, my goggles say Covert Status," said Bernie.

Alph and Digit stopped for a moment.

"Does it say Neutral?" asked Alph.

"Yeah, what does it mean?"

"It should read Neutral when you're not operating undercover," said Alph. "Try placing your finger on the side of the goggles and saying, Covert Menu."

Bernie did as she was told. The display on her goggles flickered for a moment and then a row of pictures of different mice scrolled in front of her vision. They were all different ages, shapes, sizes, and colors. Male and female. The clothes they wore depicted different careers, from mechanic's coveralls to an elegant elderly mouse wearing a ballroom gown. It was like looking at an entire world of mice.

"Wow," said Bernie.

"Oh, wow, doesn't even begin to describe it." Digit chuckled. "Wait until the next part. See those code numbers listed underneath the photos? Go ahead and pick one of the pictures and say it out loud."

Bernie didn't know which one to pick. But after a moment she decided on a frumpy-looking mousewife wearing a mauve sweatshirt with an iron-on duck. She had frizzy hair and glasses and made Bernie giggle.

"Three seven two six," said Bernie, reciting the code at the bottom of the photo.

Her glasses flickered again and the words *Covert Status: Neutral* changed to *Enhanced Reality*.

Bernie didn't feel any differently. But the reactions from Alph and Digit were immediate. Both of them chuckled when they looked at her.

"Great choice!" commended Alph.

"I don't feel anything," said Bernie.

"Come over here and take a look at yourself," said Digit. He motioned her over to the locker on the wall. Bernie saw that a small mirror had been installed on the inside of the door. When she saw herself, she gasped and then laughed out loud. She looked exactly like the photo. She was thirty years older and at least that many pounds heavier. When she moved her head, the frumpy mousewife did, too. She tried making faces. The disguise she wore was so perfectly attuned to her face that it captured the subtlest changes.

"This is amazing!" said Bernie. "How is it possible?"

"Nanotechnology and motion capture," said Digit. "The goggles emit a field of microscopic projectors that cover your entire body, fooling the outside viewer into thinking they're seeing something else. Advanced motion-capture animation does the rest. I have to admit, when Gadget presented my team with the concept we thought it couldn't be done. Took us almost a decade to perfect the tech," said Digit.

Bernie thought about how fun it would be to go home and fool her parents. She could look like practically anybody!

"Just say, *Return to Normal* and you'll be back to your old self," said Alph. "Oh, and also, when you're not using goggles, put them in sleep mode. If you're ever captured or discovered, they'll just look like ordinary goggles and nobody but you can turn them on or off once the goggles have recognized your fingerprint."

Bernie did as she was told and her Covert Status returned to Neutral. Wearing the goggles made her really feel like a Mouse Watch agent.

As they continued to follow the blue light down the hall toward orientation, Bernie noticed that some of the glass offices had windows that were grayed out so that nobody could see inside. Alph noticed her glance and said quietly, "Top secret."

Bernie nodded. Of course, there had to be things that were on a "need to know" basis. Right now, she wasn't someone who "needed to know." But she vowed to herself then and there that someday she would be, someday she would be an agent who was allowed to know all the secrets.

The blue line that they followed ended at a set of gleaming bay doors. As they approached, a tiny red laser scanner swept over Alph and Digit. After recognizing them as appropriately authorized agents, the white doors slid open and Bernie was ushered into a large conference room filled with other young mice. Most of them wore simple yellow jumpsuits unadorned with any badges.

A sign that was projected above a podium read, INITIATION AND PROMOTION CEREMONY.

Are those other new recruits? Bernie thought. She wondered where they got the jumpsuits, and why she didn't have one. *Did I miss something?*

The thought that she was not the only new recruit stung a little. She'd been fantasizing about the one-on-one training scenario with Gadget so many times that it was hard to let that idea go.

"Well, here we are," said Digit. "Alph and I will be around . . . I'm sure we'll run into you before too long. Any questions before we go?"

"Wait, you're leaving?" asked Bernie, feeling nervous. "I was kind of hoping that you'd . . . well . . . stick around for a bit."

"Oh, we're not invited to the Initiation and Promotion Ceremony," said Alph. She patted Bernie's shoulder and looked at her kindly. "We'll catch up with you later. Don't worry, Bernie, you'll be fine."

"I . . . I know that," retorted Bernie, feeling defensive. She wriggled out from under Alph's paw, not wanting to appear weak. Then she felt bad and softened her tone. "I'm sorry. I just . . . never mind," she said, her voice barely above a whisper.

Alph and Digit exchanged knowing glances as if each of them remembered the days of being intimidated new recruits. "Right-o," said Digit with a wink. "Keep your chin up. See ya around, rookie."

After they left, Bernie found a seat that was a little bit apart from the other young mice and tried to settle her racing nerves. She was both excited and nervous, secretly feeling afraid that somehow there might have been a mistake and that she wasn't really supposed to be there.

The Watch doesn't make mistakes, she told herself. *They're experts. They know what they're doing.*

But even though the thoughts were encouraging, they still didn't calm her nerves. She still didn't see how the lame videos she'd posted would have been enough to get their attention. She also wasn't dressed in the yellow jumpsuits that the other mice wore, and if they were new recruits like she was, then why didn't she have one, too?

Insecure thoughts raced around in her head as the

lights in the room dimmed, signaling that everyone should take his or her seat. Bernie scanned the crowd and figured that there had to be at least forty or fifty new recruits. Some of them, she noticed, seemed to already be friends and were chatting happily together.

I wonder if they just met or if they already knew each other, Bernie thought.

She didn't want to admit it, but it was hard not to wish she had someone to share the experience with, too. A pang of loneliness washed over her, and she tried not to think about all the hours she'd spent by herself at home. The only people in her life she'd had to talk to for the last few years were her parents, and now they were miles and miles away.

Doesn't matter, she reminded herself, *you're here. Be tough. You can do this. You'll show them that you're no mistake.*

And, fortunately, she didn't have to dwell on it much longer. A spotlight hit the podium.

The room fell silent.

And then, the mouse Bernie had most hoped to see, her idol, appeared as if out of nowhere on the stage. She'd seen her countless times before on the posters in her room. She'd read all the books about her adventures. She'd watched all the internet footage that displayed her incredible inventions and heroic deeds.

It was Gadget Hackwrench!

CHAPTER 9

Only it wasn't *exactly* her.

It was a hologram. This version of Gadget glowed a faint, iridescent blue. Bernie noticed that it flickered a little bit around the edges.

When Gadget began to speak, at first Bernie thought that the hologram might be linked to some kind of live streaming video. But then Bernie felt a little disappointed. It was obviously a prerecording.

"Hi, everybody!" the Gadget hologram said in her chipper, always optimistic voice. She waved to the roaring, applauding crowd. Bernie was amazed at how realistic Gadget looked and felt another twinge of disappointment that she wasn't there in real life. Before the clapping ended, the prerecorded Gadget began to speak.

"Sorry I couldn't be there in person," she said, pushing her trademark goggles back on her head. "I'm in the middle of creating a brand-new invention, one that will really give us an edge on the R.A.T.S." She winked. "Just wait. You guys are gonna have so much fun with this. I can't tell you too much right now, but let's just say that soon, antigravity won't be something only seen in sci-fi movies."

Oohs and *aahs* of appreciation echoed through the crowd. Bernie could hardly believe what she was hearing. Had Gadget really done what even the human scientists couldn't imagine being possible? Her mind reeled. *Antigravity? Really?*

"Today we have the privilege of advancing a group of students who have successfully completed basic training. From this point onward, those of you who are chosen will never wear a yellow jumpsuit again."

Cheers erupted.

Bernie felt a surge of relief. Evidently, the yellow jumpsuits were for recruits already in training. The fact that she hadn't been given one yet was okay. She glanced around at the cheering students and noticed something else, something that made her heart skip a beat. None of the other mice were dressed in civilian clothes. As far as she could tell, she was the only new recruit in the whole bunch!

"Those of you who have graduated to Level One will be receiving new uniforms that designate the department to which you've been assigned. As usual, it will be black for special ops, gold for research and development, and crimson for interior security. For those who will be leaving us, we thank you for the time you've put in and wish you well on your civilian journey," said Gadget. "As a souvenir of your time spent with us, you will receive two items. The first one is a certificate of appreciation, celebrating your initiate status. Remember, it was no small thing to be chosen. You were singled out because you are special, and we want you to remember that. Not everyone is suited for the Mouse Watch, but it doesn't mean that you can't do good wherever you are."

Polite applause filled the chamber.

Civilian journey? thought Bernie. *So, not everyone who is recruited makes it into the Watch. No pressure . . .*

Her stomach lurched uncomfortably and beads of sweat popped up on her forehead. Apparently, getting a recruitment letter didn't mean what she'd thought it meant. It didn't mean that you were automatically "in." It just meant you got an audition.

What if I'm not able to make it through basic training, what then? The very thought of returning home in disgrace after everything she and her parents had been through made her feel like throwing up.

Bernie gritted her teeth and tried to focus on the positive. *That's not going to happen. I'm going to make it. I'm not going to be a failure. No way.*

Hologram Gadget proceeded to ask all the recruits who

had passed basic training to stand. As she read down the list, Bernie's dismay grew more pronounced. Out of the assembled crowd only five . . . *five* . . . recruits advanced to Level One!

Bernie could see the disappointment on the faces of the mice in yellow jumpsuits who hadn't been chosen. They all clapped and cheered like good sports for the lucky few who had advanced. From a hidden compartment, five pedestals rose, each bearing a jumpsuit in the color of the various classifications that the Level One agents had been assigned.

"Will Jordan Swishtail, Maggie Whiskerfoot, William Nosetwitch, Carlie Fleetbottom, and Bryan Fuzzyears, please approach the podium."

The five recruits were all beaming with pride as they approached the podium and received their individually designated uniforms. Bernie was filled with envy as she watched them each take the one that bore his or her name on the lapel and display it for the crowd to see.

"Congratulations and welcome to the Watch," said Gadget proudly.

Several agents emerged from the back of the room. Bernie watched as they passed small, beautiful boxes to all of the recruits. As the boxes were opened, more excited *oohs* and *aahs* filled the chamber. Bernie craned her neck, trying to see what was inside of them.

Gadget held up her wrist, displaying a glowing smart watch. Bernie could see that on its face was an animated mouse, clad in a black, silver-trimmed special ops uniform.

"This is the second item I mentioned in addition to your certificates. The watches you have received are more than just a souvenir of your time spent with us. Each of them is equipped with many unique features, including two-way communication, defensive weaponry, and some secret features that you'll no doubt discover soon," Gadget said with a wink. "Study the instruction manual well." Then she added, "Should we ever need to contact you, you'll get an alert. But feel free to also use them to stay in touch with us and the new friends you've made here. We all wear them, and you will forever be part of our family."

Applause filled the room. Bernie felt something in her stir at the idea of being part of this family, of belonging.

She really wanted one of those watches for herself!

An agent wearing a red uniform stepped out from the wings and ushered the fledgling agents backstage. When the applause died down, Gadget's hologram motioned for everyone to take their seats.

"The rest of you might not have become agents, but you will always be remembered by the Watch. Be prepared and vigilant. Our agents might contact you in a time of need.

"Now, one more matter of business to attend to,"

she said, her eyes glittering. "Our new recruits! Would Bernadette Scampersky please join me on the stage?"

All eyes in the room watched as Bernie, looking pale, rose from her seat and walked up to the stage. Her knees shook a little but she forced herself to look calm and resolute as she walked up to approach the image of her greatest heroine.

Gadget smiled. And even though she was a hologram, Bernie felt the encouraging warmth that radiated from her. The hologram turned back toward the crowd and said, "Please give Bernie a warm welcome!"

Then, in unison, the entire group responded with loud, ringing voices, "*Every part of a watch is important, from the smallest gear on up. For without each part working together, keeping time is impossible. We never sleep. We never fail. We are there for all who call upon us in their time of need. We are the MOUSE WATCH!*"

Everyone applauded and Bernie blushed from the tip of her nose to the end of her tail.

So she *was* the only new recruit! A warm, fuzzy feeling bloomed inside her. She was special after all. She was small but mighty. And she was going to ace basic training and become a full-fledged member of the Mouse Watch even if it meant breaking every bone in her body!

"Welcome to the Watch, Bernie," Gadget said. "And now, will Jarvis Slinktail join me onstage as well?"

Bernie's heart dropped. *What?*

A large figure emerged from the back of the room and made its way toward the stage. For a moment, Bernie thought he was a giant mouse, taller and broader than any mouse she had ever seen.

Then everyone, including Bernie, gasped.

As Jarvis stepped into the light, Bernie realized that he wasn't a mouse at all.

Jarvis was a *rat*.

He wore a big, tattered red hoodie, and had a large flop of blond hair that fell over one of his eyes. He positioned himself awkwardly on Gadget's other side. Bernie noticed that he kept his gaze on the floor and didn't meet anybody's eyes.

Then, as Bernie's shock began to wear off, another realization struck. She was no longer the only recruit standing with Gadget on that stage.

"Mice of the Watch," Gadget said, apparently unaware that there was also a rat in their midst. "I'm pleased to introduce our second new recruit. Please welcome Jarvis!"

Murmurs rippled through the crowd. They recited the Mouse Watch anthem for a second time—though distinctly not as loudly or as energetically as the first.

As the tall rat blushed and shifted uncomfortably, Bernie couldn't help but think, *The only thing worse than there being another new recruit is another new recruit who's a rat!* She sized him up from the other side of the stage.

It had to be a joke. Gadget could be funny and playful. Maybe she was just trying to end the assembly on a surprise note?

Bernie scanned the room. Nobody was laughing. She glanced back at Jarvis. Maybe he was just a really, really big mouse? But one look at the distinctive snout and long, thick tail told her otherwise.

Then a thought occurred to her, one that sent a shiver down her spine. Would it . . . could it . . . possibly be that he was the one the Candroid mentioned?

Was Jarvis Slinktail a R.A.T.S. operative masquerading as a new recruit? If so, they were all in trouble . . . and Bernie, Alph, and Digit were the only ones who knew.

CHAPTER 10

D r. Thornpaw's metal claws gripped the rails of a rusted balcony.

The platform on which the rodent stood was bolted to the dripping brick and tile walls, the remains of an abandoned subway station that was now his secret laboratory.

The doctor surveyed the decrepit, sprawling chamber below in greedy anticipation of the glorious moment to come. After years of attempts, this was finally "it."

It was time to see if the secret formula he'd created would finally work.

On the floor of the lab, next to an array of tables filled with beakers, test tubes, and Jacob's ladders, was a series of cells with iron doors. Each of them contained one of his numerous experimental subjects. Most of them were permanently damaged in one way or another from his previous encounters with them, and the echoes of their pitiful moans filled the room.

Dr. Thornpaw thought the sounds made excellent background music while he conducted his cruel studies.

The doctor's one good eye glinted as he watched the latest subject, Ernie, being dragged out of the farthest cell and then roughly placed into a chair that had been outfitted with leather restraining belts.

The terrified elderly man whimpered as he was strapped in. Dr. Thornpaw, oblivious to Ernie's pathetic struggles, lifted a bullhorn. After switching it on with a squeal of feedback that made everyone, including the laboratory assistants, cringe, the doctor croaked in an amplified voice, "Please make yourself comfortable, Ernie. This test will only take a moment."

"Will I be able to go home afterward?" Ernie whimpered.

"Yes, yes, of course," lied Dr. Thornpaw. "Now then, Number Six, will you please administer the spray?"

The assistants, a mob of large rats dressed in identical lab coats, each had a number inscribed onto their right pockets. They also wore red rubber gloves and matching welding goggles, something that the doctor insisted was practical as well as orderly. It was satisfying when everyone matched.

"Um, boss?" A squat rat with the number eight on his pocket raised a paw.

"Yes, Number Eight?" said Dr. Thornpaw.

Number Eight shifted his feet and gulped nervously. He glanced at the other lab rats and then said, "Uh, we were all talking—"

"Oh, you were, were you? Talking? I don't pay you to talk, Number Eight," croaked Thornpaw.

"Yes, y-yes, I know that, boss." Number Eight looked like he was about to faint from fear. He knew he was treading on dangerous ground. "But, well, we were just wondering if we could, well, you know, wear something else? These lab coats are kind of scratchy and the rubber gloves stick to our paws."

Dr. Thornpaw glared at him with his one good eye. In a carefully controlled voice, he replied, "Number Eight, you know that I insist upon everyone matching while at work. Once our mission is accomplished, you will be allowed to dress as befitting the occasion. For now, I must insist that you carry on doing your job without further distractions, is that clear?"

The doctor's low, dangerous tone was not lost on the squat rat. Many of his colleagues had been subjected to terrible punishments for asking questions. The fact that he wasn't dead already suggested Thornpaw was in an unusually good mood.

"Right, boss. Of course, boss," said Number Eight, nervously saluting. Then, after hesitating again for a moment, he timidly raised his hand.

"Something else, Number Eight?" Thornpaw's voice grated even more than usual.

"Um, so that means wearing flip-flops is definitely out?"

Dr. Thornpaw pressed a remote control in his pocket. A trapdoor slid open beneath Number Eight, and the rat disappeared with a loud scream. The door slid shut, muffling the sound. There was a hiss, and then a stench emanated from the cracks in the floor. Number Eight was now hurtling far below the subway system, never to be seen again.

"Anybody else need a costume change?" asked the doctor.

All the numbered rats scurried to continue with their duties.

The fate of Number Eight was a good reminder that it was easier to go along with whatever the doctor wanted than to resist.

Number Six, a mottled rat with a single, yellow fang, retrieved a modified human-size bug sprayer that had been bolted onto a small cart. It wobbled precariously as he wheeled it over to the old man. Once it was in position, two other assistants helped him raise it by cranking a small gear that ratcheted it up to the proper angle.

"Now, Ernie, when my assistant pulls the trigger, I want you to breathe in the vapor," said Thornpaw.

"Is . . . is it safe?" stuttered Ernie, eyeing the trapdoor that Number Eight had recently fallen into.

"Of course it is," lied Thornpaw again. "It smells like cheese. You like the smell of cheese, don't you, Ernie? Everyone does. Nice, safe, good-smelling cheese." He liked lying. It was fun to watch how readily the victims seized upon what he said, believing it to be true that everything would be pleasant again soon. Humans liked to believe that everything would be okay.

Fools.

The old security guard didn't see the look that passed between assistants Number Six and Number Three. It was a look that said they'd heard this same exact speech given to every single one of the other experiment subjects.

"Administer the formula, Number Six," commanded Thornpaw.

At the signal, all of the rat assistants placed gas masks over their snouts.

After putting on his own, Number Six took careful aim.

Ernie looked even more nervous.

"Hey . . . don't I get one of those?" he asked hopefully, indicating the masks with a jerk of his head.

Number Six pulled the trigger.

An orange particle cloud shot out of the sprayer, misting over the top of Ernie's head. As the particles drifted downward, a familiar scent filled the room, one that the old man recognized immediately.

"Mmmmm. You're right! It does smell like melted cheese!" said Ernie. "Is this some kind of new air freshener?"

The old man looked relieved as he breathed in the vapors. "Here I thought you were up to something, and all you were doing was trying to freshen up the place," Ernie said happily. "Although I have to say, I'm not too sure it will be a big seller. Not many people would want . . . would want . . ."

Ernie's voice grew thick and distant.

Thornpaw's eye narrowed, studying the old man's reaction. He glanced at the clock.

Ten seconds.

Ernie didn't turn blue.

Twenty seconds.

Ernie wasn't screaming with boils all over his arms and face.

Thirty seconds.

The old man's eyes hadn't fallen out of his head. This was a first!

A few seconds more, thought Thornpaw.

Finally, at exactly forty-five seconds from the moment Ernie had first inhaled the chemical formula, his blue eyes changed color. The rats all stared, amazed, as the human's eyes faded first to white, then to green, and then they began to glow, radiating with an unearthly, sickly yellow color.

Thornpaw wanted to scream in triumph. It had taken months of planning and prep work, but finally, his plan was coming together.

First came the spying. Months of watching the Mouse Watch drone fleet for one tiny mistake. And eventually it had happened. The minute that drone crashed, Dr. Thornpaw and his league of minions went into action. Before the pilot could radio back to headquarters for help, the doctor had moved in to swipe it. The Mouse Watch agent was now officially "Missing in Action," and Dr. Thornpaw had a convenient delivery vehicle.

Just as he predicted, inside the drone was a healthy supply of Gadget Hackwrench's famous Sleep Spray. All the doctor had to do was chemically manipulate it into something else—something useful!

And now, after months of failed experiments, he had finally done it.

Gadget Hackwrench was brilliant.

But in the doctor's estimation, she was nothing compared to his own genius.

Thornpaw controlled those feelings of triumph and didn't allow a smile to cross his twisted face. Instead, the half machine, half rodent picked up the megaphone and growled, "Release the human."

The lab rats unbuckled the straps that held Ernie in the chair.

"Number Fifteen, start the music. Number Seven bring over that Bunsen burner," Thornpaw commanded.

The assistant did as she was told, approaching a nearby table and removing a small, burning stove from beneath a bubbling beaker, while Number Fifteen produced a record player.

"Ernie, stand up!" said Thornpaw.

The old man didn't hesitate, but leaped to his feet like a marionette pulled upward on a string and said in a very dull voice, "Yes, Doctor."

"Very good," said Thornpaw. "Now, Ernie, I want you to do something for me."

"Yes, Doctor," said Ernie.

Thornpaw paused. This was the true test. If this final part of the experiment worked, then the doctor would finally turn the tables around. No longer would rats be subjected to the whims of humans. No longer would they be forced underground.

If this next test worked, it was the first step toward a brand-new world. It would be a world of the doctor's own imagining, a world run by rats, where humans would finally know how it felt to be on the bottom of the food chain.

"Number Seven, please start the music," said Thornpaw.

The assistant did as she was told. She placed the needle

on the record. After a couple of pops and crackles, the ominous and familiar strains of Bach's Toccata and Fugue filled the air.

Perfect, thought the doctor, finger-conducting an imaginary orchestra. He loved sophisticated torture music. Now, if all went well, the subject wouldn't resist the next command.

Thornpaw paused. Then, after taking a deep breath, he said, "Place your hand in the fire, Ernie."

Without hesitation, Ernie thrust his hand directly into the Bunsen burner.

He didn't so much as flinch as the smell of burning, blistering flesh filled the air.

Thornpaw relished the moment, realizing that he hadn't been wrong, that the final test had been passed.

The doctor had finally perfected the formula.

And with it, the R.A.T.S. would conquer the world.

CHAPTER 11

At first, the voice Bernie heard when she woke up sounded like her mother's. Up until that moment, she'd been in the middle of a very turbulent dream. It had started with a giant, hoodie-wearing rat with two heads stealing her parents' smartphone. Then the dream had turned into a nightmare as she'd heard her brother Brody crying out for help, and Bernie had been unable to find him, to do anything other than remain frozen where she stood. She'd then heard her mother screaming at her, "Move! Bernie, get up and move!"

"I'm up, Mom! Calm down!" Bernie mumbled as she forced herself to wake from the terrible dream. But when the voice continued speaking, she realized right away that not only was it not her mother, but it wasn't alive. It was a robot.

Wake up, recruit! said the voice. Bernie looked around

to find the source and saw the Candroid, with its two brightly lit LED eyes staring down at her, in her room. For a second, she was disoriented. Where was she? But then the past twenty-four hours came rushing back, and she remembered that shortly after the welcome ceremony she'd been shown to her new quarters at Mouse Watch HQ. She'd been so exhausted she'd meant to take a short nap.

Apparently, she'd slept much longer than she'd intended to.

She glanced around her room, taking in all the strange new details. The walls were smooth and white. Running through the center of each wall was the same faintly glowing stripe of blue light that ran through most of the facility. There were also some simple, modern furnishings: a desk with round corners, an ergonomically curved chair, and a dresser. Recessed lights were hidden in the ceiling above the bed and in the small, private bathroom.

The only other item in the room was the Candroid, and as far as Bernie could tell, it didn't seem too happy to find her still asleep. Bernie wasn't sure whether or not she was actually supposed to reply to the artificial life-form, but then decided that she might as well acknowledge it.

"Okay, I'm up," she said. "Where do I go? What do I do?"

"You have a busy day ahead," said the robot. "Breakfast is the first thing on your list. What would you like to eat?"

Bernie's stomach rumbled. It had been so long since

she'd last eaten! Not only that, but because her family usually foraged for meals, she couldn't remember the last time someone had asked her *specifically* what she wanted to eat.

She thought about it for a moment, thinking of all the human food she'd ever smelled and wished she could have tried. She snapped her fingers, remembering a time she'd seen a small child eating something that smelled delicious.

"Peanut butter toast!" said Bernie.

The Candroid played light jazz from a speaker somewhere in its chest cavity while it processed her request. Then it walked over to a hatch in the wall of her bedroom and removed a small tray.

A delicious scent of warm toasted peanut butter filled the air.

Bernie's mouth watered as she took the treat from the robot. When she chomped into the creamy, crispy toast her tail swished with happiness. It was by far the best breakfast she'd ever eaten!

She'd just finished her last mouthful and was about to request a second piece when the Candroid said, "Your presence is required in room one seventy-seven. You have ten minutes, Ms. Skampersky." Then the voice changed to that of a military drill sergeant.

"MOVE, MOVE, MOVE!"

Ten minutes!

"Yes, ma'am! Sir! Or . . . whatever you are!" Bernie exclaimed as she leaped into action.

She found several yellow jumpsuits in her closet and was surprised to see her name—B. Skampersky—stitched on all of them. She also noticed that the sparkly pink suitcase had been unpacked and stowed neatly in the corner.

Good riddance to that, thought Bernie. She decided that to keep it in pristine condition, it would have to remain untouched in that closet for the entire time she was training. Her mom would be pleased to see that it wouldn't have a scratch on it.

Each yellow jumpsuit was sealed in special plastic that kept the uniform immaculately clean, pressed, and wrinkle-free. Glancing around at all that had happened while she was asleep, she could only assume that it had been the Candroid that had done it all.

Amazing.

After peeling away the plastic on one of the jumpsuits, she tried to take a very quick shower. It went a little longer than she'd intended because there were perfectly positioned water jets installed in the walls, ceiling, and floor. The water that sprayed from them was deliciously warm and lightly scented with a special soap that smelled like lilacs and made her fur feel wonderful.

After that, she styled her bright blue hair to its full

height using some hair gel that had been supplied, along with a brand-new toothbrush and toothpaste, and then, knowing she was definitely running late, she raced out the door with her new goggles and only seconds to spare.

She arrived at room 177 breathing hard. And even though she was one minute and fifteen seconds late, everybody noticed.

That was because the only one already there was Jarvis. The lanky teenage rat glanced at the digital clock mounted up on the wall of the gleaming conference room as Bernie made her breathless entrance. He was also wearing a yellow jumpsuit—one that had been outfitted with a hood.

Then, to her surprise, he offered his paw.

"We haven't officially met," he said shyly. "I'm Jarvis. You're Bernie, right?"

Bernie didn't shake his paw at first. The terrible dream she'd had the night before came rushing back, and she was reminded again about the awful Saturday her brother had been taken away from her. She glanced at his paw and then back up to his face, noticing that the flop of blond hair failed to hide the earnest expression in his eyes.

"Riiiight," she said awkwardly, gripping his paw and releasing it quickly.

She felt really uncomfortable shaking hands with a rat. She knew that she wasn't the most sociable person in the world, but if it had been anyone else she felt she could have mustered up at least a little bit of niceness. The fact that Jarvis was a rat really bothered her. Not only that, but what if he *was* the secret R.A.T.S. operative in the base? Why was he here and how could he possibly be trusted?

Well, I guess they know what they're doing, thought Bernie. *Who am I to question? If they've decided to make him a recruit and he's obviously a rat, then Gadget must think he's okay.*

She shot Jarvis a quick sideways glance. *Doesn't mean that I have to like or trust him, though.*

A familiar voice interrupted the awkward moment. Alph came bounding in through the door in the back of the room, gesturing broadly.

"Welcome, new recruits!" she said happily. Then she added, "You're not as big a crowd as our last batch, but it's quality over quantity, am I right?"

Bernie thought about how many yellow jumpsuits she'd seen yesterday. Was it unusual that there were only two recruits rather than dozens? She was about to ask, when Alph reached out to Jarvis, shaking his paw.

"You must be Jarvis! Welcome! My name's Alph, I'll be your tactical trainer."

Jarvis took her paw and shook it. Bernie wasn't sure, but she thought he looked grateful to have been welcomed so warmly. Alph turned to Bernie and offered a friendly wink.

"Good to see you again, Bern!"

"Hey, Alph!" said Bernie. She was relieved to see a familiar face.

Alph grinned back at her as she walked over to a panel on the wall and waved her paw over a scanner. As a huge high-definition flat screen descended from the ceiling, she motioned for Bernie and Jarvis to take seats at the conference table.

"You've each been chosen for specific reasons. You both have skills that have been noticed by the Watch. The testing that you'll undergo in the upcoming weeks will determine if you can integrate those skills into our organization," said Alph. "For example, one of you is particularly good with hacking codes. In fact, your abilities registered so far off the scale, we'd never seen anything like it."

Bernie felt a glow of pride. She was about to thank Alph for the compliment when the red-haired mouse turned to Jarvis and smiled. "You really have a spectacular gift, Jarvis."

The lanky rodent blushed.

Bernie tried to keep her jaw from hitting the floor.

"Wait," she said. "I thought I was here for that . . ."

Alph chuckled. "Well, you're good at puzzles, that's true. After all, you figured out the one on the recruitment gear. However, that's not the reason we chose you."

She turned toward the big flat screen and said, "Pull up video eleven forty-three, alpha plural alpha."

The hi-def screen flared to life, and seconds later, security-cam footage of Bernie's ill-fated zip-line attempt with Poopie appeared. Bernie watched, her cheeks flushed with embarrassment, as the incident replayed in front of Jarvis and Alph, both of whom chuckled when she and Poopie crashed into the trash can at the end.

"Ouch!" said Alph with a laugh.

"Were you okay?" asked Jarvis.

"Broke my leg," mumbled Bernie. She was feeling embarrassed, confused, and angry because her massive fail had been seen by the Mouse Watch. She'd thought that the footage had been destroyed when her parents' smartphone had broken, but apparently, the Watch had access to her neighborhood's security-camera footage.

Alph noticed that Bernie looked angry, and she smiled good-naturedly. "What you did back there took an incredible amount of courage. It's one of the values we rely on here."

Bernie felt a little better but not much. "Yeah, but I blew it at the end."

"Doesn't matter," said Alph with a shrug. "Here we can train you to be better at doing things like that, but we can't teach someone to have guts."

Alph gestured at the flat screen and said, "Play video one."

The conference room lights automatically dimmed.

Then, after a few seconds of black on the screen, a low, ominous chord vibrated across the room.

BOOOM! A fiery explosion filled the screen.

A Mouse Watch recruit came flying toward the camera in slow motion holding a helpless mouseling that he was rescuing from the fiery blaze. A techno beat began its rhythmic thumping, accompanied by a pulsing synthesized track.

Then a montage of dynamic training exercises played on the screen. A woman's voice, low and intense, described all the qualities that the Mouse Watch stood for and their storied history, from the early days of the Rescue Rangers to Gadget's incredible elite spin-off organization.

"We need a special kind of mouse," said the voice. "One that is ready to push themselves to the limit." Bernie watched as a team of cadets rappelled down a cliff, sharks circling in the waters below. "A mouse that will rush into danger if it means helping someone in need."

Bernie saw that there was a small boat with an old fishermouse stranded in shark-infested waters. The intrepid mice grabbed the helpless old rodent and, after strapping him to a gurney, towed him carefully skyward, up, up, up to the waiting drone, narrowly avoiding the snapping jaws of the great white sharks below. The relieved fishermouse thanked his rescuers, who nodded and gave him an encouraging pat on the back.

"We want mice who care, mice who want to see the world become a better place. From the small scale . . ."

Two agents helped a stranded bird with a broken wing, not concerned in the slightest that once it healed it might grab their tails in its beak and fly away. Despite its size, the animal was afraid and needed help, and they showed no hesitation.

"To important global issues . . ."

There were digital simulations, with mice wearing haptic gloves and virtual-reality gear. There were mock intelligence briefings with genius-level code-breaking classes.

Then a spinning globe appeared, with digital bubbles popping up all over the world. They were text messages, each one sent from a Mouse Watch agent back to HQ. Bernie tried to read as many of them as she was able to, but they popped up so fast, she could only make out a few of the messages.

Rescued a lost human child, mission accomplished.

Stopped a R.A.T.S. agent from infiltrating Buckingham Palace, ready for next assignment.

Helped a hurt Andean condor mend its wing. Hatchlings have their mother back.

Need more intel on something called KRYPTOS, please advise.

The voice continued, "Every sixty seconds a Mouse

Watch agent reports in from somewhere around the world. The missions can be as simple as helping an elderly person cross the street to thwarting dangerous R.A.T.S. operatives. No matter what the need, there's an agent nearby to answer the call for help."

The montage ended with rapid-fire clips of agents doing good deeds all over the world, from helping build a well for a thirsty village to capturing criminals. The images sped by faster and faster, ending with a thunderclap and the silhouette of a dozen new recruits standing on a mountaintop, all looking tough and fearless.

When the footage was over and the lights in the conference room came back up, Jarvis and Bernie spontaneously applauded. They couldn't help it. The entire presentation had left Bernie feeling excited, moved, and inspired. These were exactly the kind of mice she wanted to be like, mice she could look up to. She was determined to try her best to live up to their expectations.

Bernie wondered how on earth she could ever become someone so incredible! She knew the Watch was good, but these guys seemed like superheroes.

Alph grinned at Bernie's awestruck expression and patted the young recruit on the back.

"You and Jarvis are going to be a team while training. It'll take some work, so we recommend learning to rely on each other's skills," she said.

Bernie bristled. She glanced at Jarvis and said quietly, "No offense, but I'd rather do this alone."

Alph shrugged. "It's not a choice, rookie."

"But he's not a mouse . . . shouldn't we be dealing with someone more trustworthy?" Bernie began, but Alph held up her hand, interrupting her.

"I don't want to hear it, rook. He's been vetted by the Watch and that's good enough for you, got it?" said Alph.

"And I'm standing right here, you know," said Jarvis quietly.

Bernie didn't apologize and she didn't make eye contact. She felt a little embarrassed at getting a lecture from Alph, but she still couldn't bring herself to accept having a rat training with her. This was supposed to be the best time of her life!

The red-haired agent gestured to a door in the back of the room and said with her clipped British accent, "If you'll both just go through that door and step onto the conveyor, you'll be taken through a brief orientation. After that, you'll be ushered to your first recruitment challenge."

She grinned at Bernie and said, "And remember what I said about having guts? Well, soon it'll be your chance to prove to us you really have them."

CHAPTER 12

Bernie wasn't exactly sure what she expected when she went through the door, but all thoughts about being upset with Jarvis immediately left her when she walked inside the mysterious room. It was mostly a flat gray color. But in the center of the room were two hydraulic arms with harnesses attached to them. Bernie had no idea what they were for until Alph handed a VR helmet and a pair of haptic gloves to each of them.

"Go ahead and strap yourselves into the simulation rigs and put on the gloves and helmets. You guys are in for one of the most amazing experiences you've ever had."

"Motion-controlled VR?" asked Jarvis as he buckled himself into the riding harness nearest to him.

Alph smirked. "This is way beyond any virtual-reality system that the humans have developed. The experience you'll get from this will be so unforgettable that you'll never think about VR the same way again. Gadget has really developed something special. You guys all set?"

"Yeah!" Bernie said excitedly. "Is it a game? Are there points?" Once again, she didn't make eye contact with Jarvis when she said this, but she was eager to compete against the rat so that she could prove she was the better candidate.

"Just follow the leader's prompts. It's a rescue simulation but that's all I'm going to tell you," Alph said with a wink.

Bernie watched as she went to a hidden panel on the wall and opened it with a quick rap of her knuckles. She pressed her hand to a sensor and the lights dimmed until the entire room was plunged into darkness.

Bernie lowered the visor on her helmet and saw a tiny cursor blinking in the corner of her view screen.

"Good luck!" said Alph. And as the senior Watcher left the room, a low, ominous drone filled the air.

Bernie's pulse quickened. Inside the gloves she wore, her paws were sweaty.

The screen went white and the droning music around her swelled. She felt the hydraulic arm that held her begin to rise off the floor, and as it did, the music seemed to go right along with it, rising, rising and then reaching a long, harmonic crescendo that made the hair on her arms and neck stand on end.

The music ended. The room shook. Then, suddenly, she

could hear and see explosions all around her as a Mouse Watch agent appeared, shouting, "Follow me, recruit! There's a massive earthquake in southern California and we need to rescue an entire city. Hurry!"

Without thinking, Bernie ran after the agent. Everything felt so real she didn't even realize that her feet were just churning in midair. As she moved, the hydraulic arm that held her responded to every movement, and the sights and sounds, along with the sensations in her fingertips, convinced her brain that what she was seeing was really happening. She could smell the burning rubber, smoke, and broken gas lines.

I've got to get there in time!

It was the only thought on her mind as she dodged falling lampposts, massive crevices in the sidewalk, and the glass from shattered windows that rained down all around her. A blast of heat singed her whiskers as a pipe burst on her right, catapulting a manhole cover thirty feet into the air. Bernie reflexively leaped out of the way in the nick of time, but a heavy piece of asphalt hit her on the left wrist and she yelped in pain.

"OW!"

"Steady, recruit!" shouted the agent. Bernie was doing her best to keep up with him, focusing on his black jumpsuit with red trim as he darted between the feet of the towering humans, all of whom were screaming and running around in a wild, uncontrolled panic.

Bernie dodged the stampeding feet and tried to keep her balance on the constantly shifting streets. She felt beads of cold sweat on her forehead, and her heart was thumping so wildly she thought it might fly right out of her chest.

It's just a simulation! She kept repeating the words over and over in her mind, but it seemed like something abstract, a thought that at that moment argued against all her senses.

The agent in front of her took a quick read of a crumbling apartment building through his goggles, his head bobbing from side to side as he scrolled through the data that was racing across his view screen. Turning to Bernie, he said, "There's a mother and her baby on the third floor. The smoke is so thick that if we don't get there in the next ten seconds, they won't make it. The elevator isn't working so you'll have to use the fire escape. GO!"

He waved Bernie to the iron stairway next to the building. Bernie raced up the stairs, which would normally be too tall for her since they were built for humans. But because her adrenaline was so high, she leaped up each one with an amazing burst of strength, surpassing what she'd have ever thought possible athletically just a few moments before.

Pretty good for a pint-size mouse, she thought proudly.

She reached the third floor and saw, to her relief, that a window was cracked open. The opening was too small for a human—but perfect for a mouse. She slipped easily inside the room.

On the screen of her goggles a small map appeared with an infrared display of the room indicating where the mother mouse and her baby were located. She launched off her hind legs toward them, but the floor gave way beneath her! Bernie grabbed on to the splintered wood, struggling not to fall down through the gaping hole and into the inferno below.

"Help!" the mother cried.

"I'm trying!" Bernie shouted through the noise of the roaring fire and snapping wood. Then, through the fire, a hulking figure appeared above her. Bernie was about to scream when a large paw extended her way.

"Grab on!" a voice called. It was Jarvis!

Bernie's heart raced. He was her partner—she was supposed to trust him. But he was a rat—and Bernie had spent her whole life distrusting rats. . . .

And then, just as she reached out her paw . . .

. . . the screen suddenly went black.

All sounds stopped.

A deafening silence filled the simulation room, punctuated by her own quick breathing. Was it over? It seemed like a strange way to end the simulation. Maybe by not immediately trusting Jarvis, she had lost?

"How'd I do?" she asked tentatively.

"What's happening?" said Jarvis.

Bernie removed her helmet, but it didn't help much. The entire room was pitch-black, and her paws were dangling in space.

"Maybe it's still part of the test," Bernie reasoned.

Jarvis's voice floated back to her out of the darkness, "I . . . don't think so. That felt like a programming glitch to me."

Her instincts told her that something was definitely "off." They really shouldn't be stopped here for so long.

"I think something's wrong," said Jarvis. "I don't like how dark it is in here! Aah! Is that a spider?"

"Calm down," said Bernie. "I'm sure it's not that big of a deal."

Bernie's ears pricked up as she heard muffled shouts coming from outside the room. And was that the sound of an alarm going off?

There was no way to tell how high she was in the darkness, but seeing no other choice, Bernie forced the buckle open on the harness. She fell for what felt like the length of an entire apartment building—which must have only been about a foot—and landed pretty gracefully on all four paws. She hoped that she was right about all this being nothing, but, just in case . . .

"Wait, where are you going? Are you leaving?" asked Jarvis. "Shouldn't we stay here until Alph gets back? What if we get caught? I don't want to get in trouble."

"I'm going to find out what's going on," said Bernie. "Come or stay, it's up to you."

Jarvis hesitated.

The fear of being left alone seemed to trump whatever fear he had about breaking the rules, and he pushed his own buckle open and followed Bernie after falling awkwardly to the ground. The two felt their way through the darkness, to the door that Alph had exited earlier.

"It's locked," said Bernie, trying the handle.

"Maybe there's another exit?" squeaked Jarvis in a high, shaky voice. "Are we trapped in here?"

Bernie couldn't help feeling a wave of satisfaction as she realized that Jarvis may have been an ace code-breaker— but he was afraid of the dark. It must have been true—she was the brave one.

"You feel the walls on your side and I'll check mine," said Bernie. "And try to be brave. We're supposed to be Mouse Watch agents, right?"

"R-right," Jarvis said hoarsely.

There were a few anxious moments of silence as they

both searched, feeling around the walls in the pitch-black and hoping to find something. At last, Bernie let out a loud "HA!" as her paw closed around the familiar shape of a door handle.

She pushed it open.

Bernie found herself back in the huge airport hangar room that she'd first entered when disembarking from the drone. Only this time, instead of the hubbub of activity that had greeted her before, the sight was completely different.

Every desk was empty.

A dim red emergency light illuminated the entire floor.

And she could tell in an instant that something was, indeed, terribly, terribly wrong.

CHAPTER 13

Bernie took in the vacant desks, the scattered papers, the numerous laptop computers in sleep mode and wondered what might have happened to prompt such a thorough and complete evacuation. And, more importantly to her, why had she and Jarvis been abandoned in the process? Wouldn't Alph or someone, anyone, at least have remembered that she and Jarvis were in the simulation room and sent an agent to let them know what was happening?

"Ummmm . . . it looks like everyone suddenly left in the middle of what they were doing," said Jarvis. "Something horrible must have happened."

Bernie glanced up at him and noticed how anxious he looked. Beneath his flop of blond hair, his brow was furrowed and he was wringing his paws.

"I guess we should look and see if anybody's around,"

said Bernie. She immediately set off to the nearest glass cubicle and headed for the laptop within. She observed that whoever had occupied this particular desk had left so quickly that whatever they were coding was partially done and that a half-eaten sandwich was left sitting on a plate.

Must have been something really bad to leave a perfectly good sandwich, she thought. "An attack of some kind?" she wondered.

"What'd you say?" asked Jarvis.

"That cheese sandwich is half-eaten and the coffee in the cup is still warm," said Bernie, touching the paper cup. Jarvis tapped the space bar on the mouse-size laptop, and a log-in screen came up.

"Great. Password-protected," she said. "So much for that idea."

"Hang on," said Jarvis, suddenly interested. Bernie watched as the lanky rat looked over the computer carefully, noting the serial number on the bottom of it and the design.

"Hmm. It's a two-terabyte peanut drive with an integrated mousewheel graphics card. Nice," he observed. Bernie noted with interest that all of the anxiety Jarvis had been feeling seemed to have disappeared. He was completely engrossed in the machine and talking half to Bernie and half to himself.

"But there's a design flaw," he said happily. "Watch."

Jarvis's nimble rat fingers flew over the keyboard, filling the password box with a series of numbers, letters, and symbols that went by so fast Bernie didn't even have time to register them. After a few seconds, he punched the ENTER key, and the laptop, with an affirming chime, let him in.

"Wow," said Bernie. She couldn't help feeling impressed.

"Oh. Um, it's nothing really," he said awkwardly. "Occam's razor."

"Acorn razor? What does shaving have to do with anything?" asked Bernie.

"Not a *razor* like shaving," said Jarvis. "It's a mathematical probability theory. William of Ockham was a Franciscan friar who said basically that the simplest answer is usually the right one."

"Actually," said the Candroid as it rolled by, "that is the law of simplicity. Occam's razor states that when deciding between two similar hypotheses, the one with fewer assumptions is usually right."

"Actually," Jarvis said, "one could argue that—"

"So, what was the simple answer to the code you were cracking?" Bernie interrupted. The Candroid rolled away.

"Cheeselover123," said Jarvis with a shrug. "Probably the password for a lot of agents around here," he said, glancing around. "Makes me kind of hungry, actually."

"How can you think about food at a time like this?" Bernie asked.

"I can think of food at any time," Jarvis confessed. "You know what sounds especially good right now? A cheese soufflé with Tabasco sauce."

"What's that?" asked Bernie.

"Heaven on a plate," said Jarvis.

"That good?" asked Bernie.

"It's the Tabasco sauce that makes it. Wish I had some right now. I live for Tabasco."

"Well, the sooner we can find out what's going on, the sooner you can get some."

The rat started searching through the file folders on the desktop, and after a few moments located one that was labeled EMERGENCY PREPAREDNESS.

"Maybe that's something?" Bernie asked.

"Could be," said Jarvis with a shrug. He clicked on the folder.

A document came up that showed a map of HQ and various emergency exits. Bernie scanned the rooms depicted on the screen.

"Not much here other than how to do basic safety drills. Fire escapes and stuff," said Bernie. "Wait. Hey, what's that one say?" She pointed at a file on the screen.

"What, that one?" asked Jarvis. "It says *Situation Room Access Code.*"

"Can you send it to me?" said Bernie.

Jarvis clicked a button, and the file appeared in the corner of her goggles' screen.

"Now, I think I remember passing a door on the tour. . . ." She snapped her fingers. "Okay, I remember where it was . . . follow me," she said to Jarvis.

"Where are we going?" he asked.

"The Situation Room. When there's a government crisis that's where the president meets with his staff. Maybe it works the same way here."

"Oh," said Jarvis.

The two followed the map down empty corridors that had until recently been bustling with activity. They would have tried the Zoom Chutes, but since Bernie hadn't been shown how to use them yet, she decided that keeping her feet on the ground would be a better idea.

When they finally got to the place that the map indicated was the Situation Room, they found it locked.

Bernie examined the solid construction of the numerical keypad. She entered the code that they'd found in the file, but nothing happened.

"Rats! I guess they changed it," said Bernie.

"I could give it a try," said Jarvis. Then he added, "You know, 'rat' isn't a bad word." He reached into his pocket and removed a small device attached to a wire. After plugging it into the side of the numerical keypad, he pressed a series of buttons, listening closely to the touch-tone sounds it made. A few seconds later, Bernie heard the bolt slide and the door click open.

"How'd you do that?" asked Bernie.

"Touch-tone locks are pretty easy to figure out. This little device looks for the keys that have been pressed most frequently and then quickly derives a pattern."

"That's a pretty fancy device," Bernie said with suspicion. "Did you swipe that off Alpha this morning? Since you're a rat, I assume you stole it."

"NO! Will you stop . . . I'm not what you think I am," he said irritably. "I made this myself."

"Well, you need to prove that to me before I'll believe it," Bernie shot back.

"And what do you think I'm doing helping you right now? Spying for the R.A.T.S.?"

Bernie didn't want to admit that she'd been wondering about that. The trouble was, Jarvis had been acting very helpful and nice. She decided to hold off on her judgment for now.

"Fine. Okay. Good job on the lock," she said, pushing the door open and cutting the conversation short. Jarvis made it aggravatingly hard to keep her guard up. If she wasn't careful, she might forget how she felt about rats and start treating him like a friend.

Inside the massive room, dozens of screens lined the

walls, each showing up-to-the-minute news broadcasts and data reports. Against one wall was a long desk with several computers, and in the middle of the room was a large gleaming conference table. This room, like the rest of HQ, showed recent signs of a hurried exit. There were papers strewn everywhere. Monitors sat blinking, waiting for the next command. The chairs around the table were askew— some were even still spinning, as if the mouse who was sitting there had only just rushed off.

"Bernie—" Jarvis started, but couldn't finish the sentence. Instead, he pointed at the screen mounted in the very center of the wall.

Bernie stared. A bespectacled mouse news anchor was speaking urgently. At the bottom of the screen in bold letters it said: *New York City under attack . . . smells delicious!*

"Sources say that the zombielike virus has already affected over three thousand people, each of whom seemed to be under some kind of mind control. Witnesses reported the scent of warm melted cheese before the victims fell into a complete stupor. Only those who are lactose intolerant seem to be immune. . . ."

The camera cut to a scene of humans walking calmly down the street in a single-file line. Like a row of ants, they walked down subway stairs and out of sight.

"Worse still, an infestation of rats has appeared almost

out of nowhere, driving people from their homes and work-places. The mayor is considering issuing a quarantine on the entire city. We will provide up-to-the-minute details as they come after this commercial break."

The anchor paused in his report, and seemingly unaware that the cameras were still on, said to someone offscreen, "That cheese smell is driving me crazy. Anybody else hungry?"

"Starving," replied Jarvis, nodding at the screen.

"Whoa," said Bernie, taking in all that she'd just seen and heard. "I'll bet the R.A.T.S. are behind this."

"Did they really say it smelled like melted cheese?" asked Jarvis. "As if I wasn't hungry enough already . . . "

"Hey, check this out," said Bernie.

Jarvis went over to where she was standing. A computer monitor with a map showed the locations of all the Mouse Watch agents and drones, indicated by each of their names appearing over a glowing red dot. The dots were spread all over a grid of New York City, but because of the clusters of dots on top of each other, it was hard to make out any individuals by name or figure out where they were precisely located.

"I wonder if they might be in the subway system?" said Bernie. "I've heard that in New York there are tunnels that go everywhere under the city."

"Seems like a good guess to me," agreed Jarvis. "Probably

trying to keep out of sight while they find out what's causing all this mayhem."

Bernie glanced back up at the news report. "A zombie virus? Seriously? It sounds so cheesy."

"Smells that way, too," said Jarvis. "Hold on, check these out."

"What'd you find?" Bernie asked.

"Look at this," he said excitedly, shoving a sheaf of papers at Bernie. She scanned the documents, all of which were labeled CLASSIFIED.

Bernie looked over the papers. They were blueprints for a secret underground transport system. It was labeled SECRET WATCHER INTERNATIONAL SEWER SYSTEM or S.W.I.S.S. Jarvis let out a low whistle.

"A secret subway system that goes all over the world, even under the oceans?" Jarvis's long tail swished excitedly.

"Gadget can do pretty much anything," said Bernie admiringly. "She's a genius, you know."

"Yeah, I know," admitted Jarvis. "It was one of the main reasons I wanted to join you guys. That, and well, I didn't like where I was very much. . . ."

But before he could say any more, Bernie spotted something.

"Ooh, look! The entrance to S.W.I.S.S. Past the cafeteria there should be a secret entrance right behind the drinking fountains. Come on!"

She was about to set off when Jarvis held up his paws.

"Whoa, whoa! What are you doing?" he asked.

"I'm gonna catch up with the Watchers. Whatever this zombie virus is, it's obviously the reason the entire headquarters evacuated in such a hurry."

"Wait a minute. If they evacuated, do you really think they'd just leave us behind? We're new recruits! We have no idea what's going on!" said Jarvis.

Bernie wheeled on him with a suspicious expression. "You know, how do I even know I can trust you? You seemed to figure those codes out awfully quickly. Almost like you got them from an organization of evil rats trying to take over the world? And now you don't want us to even try to help? If you're hiding something . . ."

Jarvis shrunk back. "Knock it off, Bernie, I'm not a spy," he said. "I was recruited because of my code-breaking and computer skills, remember?"

"I remember," said Bernie. It still stung that she hadn't been chosen for that reason. "By the way, I'm totally watching you," she added fiercely. "The only reason we're working together is because we have to. Don't start thinking we're friends or anything like that."

Jarvis nodded, but he looked hurt.

"Fine. Yeah, I get it," he mumbled. "The rat is always the villain. Like I haven't heard that a million times before."

"Whatever," said Bernie dismissively. Deep down, she knew that Jarvis was unlike any preconceived idea she'd ever had about rats. He was, after all, the first one she'd ever met. He was actually kind of nice, in a nerdy sort of way. And it's not like mice were beating down her door to be friends. It might be nice . . .

Stop that! Bernie warned herself. She wasn't about to let her guard down and allow a rat to jeopardize her chances of becoming a real Mouse Watch agent. *You are NOT friends. Just get on with the mission. Prove to the Mouse Watch what you can do.*

She turned on her paws and marched off in the direction of the S.W.I.S.S. terminal indicated on the map. Jarvis, seeing that the choice was between staying there alone or following after, pulled his hood up, and after shoving his paws deep in his pockets, ran along behind her.

CHAPTER 14

Bernie ran toward the secret area indicated on the blueprints on her goggles screen, first dashing past the cafeteria, which still had the delicious aroma of lunch—a buffet of truffle macaroni and cheese—wafting from it. She scurried past the locker room that led to the gym and workout areas and noticed that, like everywhere else, it was completely empty and abandoned.

What had made all the agents in the Watch leave in such a hurry? Shouldn't there be a procedure for sending agents to a crisis that was more orderly and organized? Would the cafeteria workers leave all that food cooking and not put it away?

Bernie reached the drinking fountains that were indicated on the blueprint well before Jarvis did. By the time he caught up, she'd already found a switch behind them that opened the secret door.

"What took you so long?" asked Bernie.

Jarvis was huffing and puffing so hard that he couldn't answer for a full thirty seconds. He just held a finger in the air, indicating for her to wait while he caught his breath.

"Too . . . much . . . time . . ." he wheezed.

"Too much time for what?" asked Bernie. "Too much time for you to catch up?"

Jarvis shook his head no, breathing hard. He continued, saying, "Too . . . much . . . time . . . playing . . . (huff, huff) . . . video games. I prefer running in virtual . . . reality. I really need a drink of water."

Bernie rolled her eyes as Jarvis took a long swig from the drinking fountain. Then, motioning for him to hurry up and follow, she led him through the entrance to the underground S.W.I.S.S. facility.

Bernie sniffed, noticing that the air had changed as she'd descended the stairs from the dry and sterile HQ to the damp underground. When she reached the bottom of the brick staircase, she saw that the room opened up into a vast, gloomy cavern. Above her were huge archways and vaulted ceilings, and in front of her was a train platform.

"Wow," said Jarvis, looking around. "This all looks really old."

"Yeah," agreed Bernie. "Hey, there's a train platform but no train. I wonder if our goggles can give us any info, like a schedule?"

They both lowered their Mouse Watch goggles. Once activated, the lenses lit up with a blue glow that cast an eerie light in the dim shadows. Bernie saw a series of pop-up balloons appear in the corner of the screen, indicating information on how to use the transport system.

STEP ONE: SUMMON TRAIN USING VOICE COMMAND. "HEY, SWISS!"

STEP TWO: STATE DESTINATION.

STEP THREE: AFTER BOARDING THE TRAIN, SELECT SPECIFIC DESTINATION FROM THE POP-UP MENU.

STEP FOUR: BUCKLE UP!

"Seems simple enough," said Bernie. Then, speaking loudly and clearly, she said, "Hey, Swiss!"

An electronic female voice with a light British accent replied from a speaker somewhere, "Coming . . ."

A low, magnetic humming noise came from the dark tunnel. Seconds later, a bright white light shone through the darkness, which, as it drew closer, revealed itself to be a gleaming tube that looked like a subway from the future.

"Whoa," said Jarvis. "It's like something out of a video game!"

As it pulled up into view, Bernie marveled at the sleek

design of all seamless curves. Like much of the Mouse Watch tech, it was brilliant white with windows tinted so dark that she couldn't get a glimpse inside. The entire train seemed to hover above the track rather than roll on wheels along a rail.

And perhaps most impressively of all, it was just the right size for a small rodent. This was no human train they would have to sneak aboard.

"It's a miniature Maglev train!" marveled Jarvis. "It's got almost no drag due to electromagnetic repulsion. I've heard about these but never seen one up close."

The door slid open, revealing a comfy-looking interior. The seats were perfectly mouse size. There was no need for a set of smaller seats hidden away in the shadows.

"After you," said Jarvis, indicating that Bernie should go first. She hopped inside and jumped into one of the ergonomically designed seats. The interior smelled clean and new as if it had come straight off the factory floor.

As soon as Jarvis boarded and sat down, Bernie instructed the A.I. interface to take them to New York City.

"Which station?" asked the voice.

Bernie and Jarvis exchanged puzzled glances. Neither one of them had thought to check the map to see where the Mouse Watch satellite headquarters might be located.

"How about the biggest station?" suggested Bernie.

"Grand Central Terminal," replied the train. "Please make sure your restraints are properly fastened. Arrival time: T minus ten minutes."

"Ten minutes to New York?" exclaimed Jarvis. "But that's imposs—"

He didn't have the chance to finish his sentence. With a sonic *BOOOM!*, the S.W.I.S.S. train shot off at such a speed, Bernie felt herself nearly flattened in her chair.

"WHOOOHOOOO!" she shouted. It was like riding the fastest motorcycle ever invented!

Jarvis appeared to feel completely different about the ride. Glancing over at the rat, Bernie noticed that his eyes were wide with terror and that his pink nose had gone completely white. His paws gripped the seat.

The train whipped around the curves in the tunnel so fast that they could hardly be felt at all. The bricks outside the tinted windows sped by in a smeary blur. A digital map was projected at the front of their seats, and Bernie watched in amazement as the red line that indicated the train's movement sped through all the states between California and New York faster than the quickest jet.

If the humans had something like this, it would change the world, thought Bernie. *A kid could have breakfast in New York and still make it to school on time in Los Angeles.*

Then, almost as quickly as the trip had begun, it was over. Bernie felt the train slow as it approached Grand

Central Terminal and a few seconds later, the door slid open and the voice said, "Arrived. Please disembark."

Bernie was still vibrating with adrenaline from the speedy trip and felt on top of the world. Jarvis, on the other hand, looked to be feeling exactly the opposite.

He was shaking so badly that it took Bernie a full five minutes to coax him out of the transport vehicle. They exited onto a platform that was positioned inside of what looked to be an old clock, festooned with giant gears and art deco detailing. The platform itself had elegant hand railings that were painted green, and the inside of the clock smelled of dust and oil.

"Are you okay?" Bernie asked him. "Wasn't that fun?"

Jarvis nodded weakly, and then, after setting his paws back on the ground, promptly ran over to a huge gear and threw up next to it. Bernie couldn't help noticing that he'd made a mess right next to a sign that said, WELCOME TO NEW YORK MOUSE WATCH HQ.

So gross. Bernie wrinkled her nose. She'd heard that rats ate things like old pizza from dumpsters and stuff like that. She would have assumed that most rats had an iron stomach. But seeing Jarvis in such a state reminded her that this rat was different. Hadn't he talked about the wonders of a baked cheese soufflé with Tabasco sauce?

The dude isn't like any rat I've ever heard of, that's for sure, Bernie thought.

Huddled next to the large clockworks, Jarvis looked absolutely miserable. In spite of her conflicting feelings, she went over and patted him on the back. Maybe it was pity or maybe it was something else. But seeing someone, anyone, in such a state brought out a bit of compassion in her.

"Hey. You all right?" she asked.

Jarvis didn't reply. As he shakily stood up from where he'd been crouching, he kept his gaze downward as if he were too embarrassed to make eye contact.

Bernie had always imagined rats to be menacing, fearsome creatures that were all claws, fangs, and bad attitude. Jarvis couldn't be further from that image, and she wondered privately if that was why he wasn't with his own kind. Could it be that he was seeking acceptance from the Mouse Watch because he, like her, didn't fit in with everyone else? It was possible they had more in common than she thought.

Maybe I should cut him a little slack, she decided.

"How come you're not feeling sick, too?" asked Jarvis weakly.

"I dunno," Bernie said with a shrug. "Good constitution, I guess."

"Small but mighty, right?" said Jarvis.

Bernie paled. Those words. Why had he chosen those words? Whatever sympathy she'd felt for Jarvis instantly melted away when she thought about her brother.

"Don't ever say that again," warned Bernie.

"Say what?" asked Jarvis, confused.

"What you just said," said Bernie.

"What? Small but mighty? I wasn't trying to insult your size. I was trying to give you a compliment!"

Bernie was too small to grab Jarvis by the collar. Instead, she leaped at him, eyes blazing, and grabbed the bottom half of his hoodie. She stared up at him, her eyes narrowed into daggers, and said in her most dangerous voice, "Only my brother can call me that. You . . . you don't have the right!"

Jarvis stared down at her with both a startled and confused expression.

"Um, okay," he said. "I'm sorry."

Bernie released him. Her hands were shaking, and she felt sick to her stomach. After a moment, Jarvis hesitantly asked, "What happened to him?"

"He died," said Bernie quietly. "A rat killed him."

Jarvis's shoulders slumped. He shoved his paws into his hoodie pockets.

After a long moment of silence, he said softly, "I know what it's like to lose someone, too."

Bernie didn't reply.

The clock chimed noon, interrupting the awkward moment. The station platform on which they'd arrived shook alarmingly, sending small bits of rubble down from the ceiling. Bernie covered her head and held on tightly to a nearby turnstile until the booming chime stopped.

"The New York station sure isn't as sturdy as the LA Union Station platform," said Jarvis shakily.

"You're telling me," said Bernie. She gazed around at the clockworks inside the Mouse Watch station. Like the Mouse Watch headquarters in Los Angeles, the entire place was deserted.

Bernie spotted a door. Maybe it led to the New York HQ, where the mice were waiting?

"Well, we might as well see if we can find someone. Come on," said Bernie.

They walked through the mouse-size door and found themselves on a balcony outside a giant golden clock. It had four faces that were arranged in a cube and was perched high in the center of a cavernous train terminal. The view from where they stood was staggering.

Instead of a busy human train station filled with chaotic activity and people rushing this way and that trying to make their trains on time, Bernie and Jarvis were met with an unsettling sight. All of the people were moving silently into one single, eerie line. They marched slowly, like robotic soldiers. A troop of rats in white lab coats shouted commands through a tiny bullhorn, their creepy voices the only sound that echoed across the terminal.

"It's like what we saw on TV," whispered Bernie. "They're all zombies."

"Yeah," agreed Jarvis. He scanned the crowd. "I don't see any Watchers, do you?"

Bernie studied the grim scene. There were no Watchers anywhere.

"If they're not here, then where did they all go?" she asked. A fluttering panic was building inside of her stomach. What if they hadn't evacuated? What if they'd been . . . taken? But who or what in the world could be so powerful that it could take out all the agents in one fell swoop?

Suddenly, a voice with a heavy Brooklyn accent interrupted them from somewhere behind them.

"Finally! You California agents took your time! We've been waiting for you."

CHAPTER 15

Bernie and Jarvis wheeled around. Standing behind them was a very tall mouse wearing a special ops jumpsuit. He had a small, pencil-thin mustache and glittering eyes. To Bernie, he seemed like the kind of mouse who had quick reflexes and an even quicker mind.

"Sorry . . . we . . . uh . . ." began Jarvis. "What I mean is . . ."

"We're new recruits from the Watch in LA," finished Bernie, offering a firm handshake. "We would have got here sooner, but we were in orientation and had to figure out how to work the S.W.I.S.S. on our own. My name's Bernie Skampersky and this is Jarvis Slinktail."

The New York agent studied them critically for a moment. Then he shook their paws and said, "Director Whiskerpaw. Sorry you're getting thrown into this mess without training. Where's your supervisor? We've been trying to get in touch with the California agents for hours. No response at all. Did you bring backup?" He glanced over their shoulders as if hoping to see more mice disembark from the train.

Bernie glanced down. "No. When we came out of the training simulation every single agent was gone. We don't know where they went, and we came here looking for answers."

"*Rats*. Must've been R.A.T.S." The agent shook his head, and Jarvis mumbled something under his breath that sounded like *It's not a bad word*. Director Whiskerpaw seemed to notice Jarvis for the first time, eyes narrowing. "Hey, wait a minute . . ."

Director Whiskerpaw was only a little shorter than Jarvis, which was saying a lot for a mouse. He was certainly one of the tallest mice Bernie had ever met. He looked up at the rat suspiciously.

"He's okay," said Bernie quickly. "He's . . ." She glanced at him. "One of us. Gadget vouches for him."

The director looked doubtful. But then, after a moment, he shrugged and said, "Well, you two better follow me. I'll take you to HQ and we'll figure out what to do with you."

He led the way toward an elevator shaft in the center of the clock. Like the rest of the interior, Bernie noticed that it seemed very old. But once she stepped through the doors into the elevator itself, she could tell right away that it was much more than it appeared to be.

There were no buttons with numbers indicating floors. Instead, there was a jet-black panel on the wall. Whiskerpaw placed his palm on the sensor, and the elevator began its smooth descent. A few seconds later, the doors slid open and Bernie was greeted with the sights and sounds of the New York headquarters. Her first impression was that it was equally impressive as the California HQ but much different in design.

Instead of gleaming white, the entire facility was gunmetal gray. Cement walls with thin, trickling waterfall treatments added to the Zen-like space. Glass-enclosed meditation gardens with stone benches were placed artfully throughout for agents working long shifts who might need a place to take a break and to recharge. Impressive technology bays were lined up against the walls, and they were all illuminated by the glow of computer screens and holo projections. Tiny drones shaped like robotic birds dove and swooped, carrying cups of coffee or data drives to any agent that summoned them. Several agents wore enhanced reality glasses and gloves that allowed them to type on the ghostly virtual keyboards that floated above their desks and to swipe the windows displayed there in the holographic screens.

"This is it," said Whiskerpaw. "You'll notice that we

have noise-dampening walls. They keep the city noise out so that the agents can concentrate on their various assignments. Otherwise, every strike of the clock or screaming siren would drive everyone crazy."

"Impressive," said Jarvis.

"We think so," said Whiskerpaw.

In the back of the room was the largest flat screen Bernie had ever seen. It was divided into several quadrants, each one depicting a different C.C. (Critter Circuit) TV camera's view around the city. Whiskerpaw led them to the screen and pointed at a few of the live streams that were displayed there.

"As you can see, we're rapidly losing the entire city. R.A.T.S. is taking over."

Incredulity gave way to rage as Bernie saw what was happening. Vermin were everywhere, sitting in cafés drinking wine and eating truffles. They were reading newspapers and wearing tiny suits and ties. They wore yoga pants and drank rat-size cups of coffee. They had tiny cell phones, possibly stolen from Mouse Watch agents. They had replaced Broadway actors with rats. The rats had taken everything for themselves, and it looked to be just the beginning.

They had to be stopped!

The director studied her carefully, then turned his gaze upon Jarvis.

"So. We have a rat in the Mouse Watch, eh? I guess it's about as likely as rats taking over Grand Central Terminal."

Jarvis looked at the floor. There was an embarrassed silence.

"Look, kid, I'm just giving you a hard time," said the director. "If you're okay by Gadget, you're okay by us. But listen." He leaned forward, suddenly serious. "The information that I'm going to share with you is for supervisor level and above. The only reason why I'm gonna let you in on it is because we're in a rough situation. We need all the help we can get." He sighed and wiped a paw over his eyes, looking suddenly tired. Then he smiled wearily and motioned for them to follow him.

Bernie felt a strange mixture of fear and elation at being given an opportunity to help out with a real Mouse Watch mission on her very first day! The elation came from years of dreaming of this very moment. But the fear part came from knowing that she had had zero training. She was going to have to put her natural skills to the test.

The director led them into a glass-enclosed conference room that had a large screen on one wall. There was a map displayed upon it. Next to the map was a digital sketch of a monster. Or a mouse. Bernie couldn't tell which.

Two tired-looking mice in uniform were already in the room, busily working on notes on digital tablets.

"Jocelyn, Jennifer, meet a couple of new recruits. This here is Bernie and Jarvis."

The two mice stopped what they were doing and greeted the newcomers.

"If we could have a moment? I'd like to get them up to speed," said the director.

"Sure, Chief," said Jocelyn.

"Yeah, we were just finishing up," said Jennifer. She shot Jarvis a curious but not unkind look on the way out of the conference room.

"Okay, where to start?" said the director, rubbing his paws together. He indicated the map. "The red lines connect all the places that are experiencing outbreaks. So far, the only common denominator is that our agents in the field identified the scent of cheddar cheese as an orange mist drifted down from the sky. Then the humans started acting strange. Moving down the sidewalks single file. Orderly. *Quiet.* Something's not right. Not right at all."

"Cheese?" asked Bernie. "Why cheese?"

The director shrugged. "Not sure. Maybe once the mist is inhaled, it exerts some kind of mind control on the humans? We don't really know." He shrugged and smiled wistfully. "Sure smells delicious, though."

"I'm actually kind of hungry," admitted Jarvis.

"How is that even possible?" asked Bernie. "Five minutes ago you were spilling your guts outside the train platform."

Jarvis shrugged helplessly. "That was then and this is now."

"There's a human-size donut in the break room. Also, we might have some leftover cheese. Help yourself," said the director.

Jarvis politely thanked him, and as he rushed off to find it, he called back, "I hope there's some Tabasco sauce!" Bernie shook her head. *Jarvis and his Tabasco sauce. Ridiculous.*

Turning to the director, she said, "When I got off the train I noticed that there were rats in white lab coats at Grand Central Terminal. They were ordering the humans around with a bullhorn."

The director frowned and jotted something down on his tablet.

"Do we know who is behind all this?" asked Bernie.

"Funny you should phrase it like that," the director said. "This is far more organized than anything R.A.T.S. has done before. Usually they are all about causing random chaos, and they tend to work alone or in small groups. This is different. It's large-scale and calculated." He tapped on the monstrous-looking police sketch that Bernie had seen earlier. It depicted a horribly deformed rat—if you could call it that. "We think R.A.T.S. might have a new ringleader—someone poised to make R.A.T.S. a threat not *just* to mice—but to all of humanity. There have been sightings of this . . . thing."

He sighed. "We're gonna need to get our hands on one of the machines that's spraying the cheese mist and send it to Gadget's secret lab. Maybe then we can figure out how it's turning the humans into zombies. I've got a tactical group of ten agents ready to go, but we could use any extra help we can get. You game?"

"You bet," said Bernie.

Jarvis trotted back in with a big piece of chocolate donut in each of his paws. He handed one to Bernie, who suddenly found that maybe she was a bit hungry herself.

"Um, just how are we supposed to capture one of those machines from the R.A.T.S.?" asked Jarvis. "I really don't know how to use any weapons."

Director Whiskerpaw laughed. "Weapons? We're not going to give two new recruits weapons on their first day."

"Oh," said Bernie, disappointed.

"Cooper!" the director shouted.

A harried-looking agent appeared at the conference room door. "Yeah, Chief?"

"Get these two new recruits over to Major Flatpaw. They're untrained, so I want them to assist the squad. We're taking to the streets in ten."

Cooper turned his tired, baggy eyes on Bernie and Jarvis. "Well, I guess there's no better teacher than first-hand experience."

CHAPTER 16

"For those of you who don't know who I am, my name is Major Flatpaw," said the brawny mouse. Bernie noted that her hair was cut in a close bob and that her shoulders and hips were as wide as she was tall. She was a walking refrigerator of a mouse.

"We have an important mission ahead of us: steal a cheese spray machine for analytical purposes. I don't have to remind you of how many different ways it could fail. The odds are stacked against us, but we are agents of the Watch and we let nothing stand in our way! Am I right?"

All of the New York agents gathered around Bernie and Jarvis shouted in the affirmative. Bernie liked this tough, no-nonsense mouse. She was a leader who she felt she could definitely follow.

Jarvis leaned over to her and whispered, "Have you ever had cheese spray from a can? It's soooo good."

Major Flatpaw marched up to a human-size digital tablet that was twice her height. She tapped the screen and a map of New York City appeared. She pinched the screen with her paws and the map zoomed in on Times Square.

"Our number one objective is to find out exactly how that spray is turning the humans into zombies and who is behind it. Judging from the recent attacks, we think that Times Square is the best place to start our investigation as it has the highest concentration of affected humans, as well as rats. Be vigilant of the strange cheddar cheese scent in the air. Somehow, it is linked to the mind control. Keep your noses down and your whiskers alert. Don't engage with any humans or rats. Your only goal is to get one of the cheese spray machines and bring it back to HQ immediately."

"I once ate a whole can of cheese spray," Jarvis again whispered to Bernie. "I was sick for days, but it was worth it!"

"Shhh," said Bernie.

"You! Sharpears!"

A young, tough-looking mouse stepped forward. "Yes, ma'am?"

"Take a team and scour the area near Broadway. Use every sensitive listening device we have and try to figure out who is giving the rats orders. Whatever you do, don't get caught."

Sharpears saluted and selected a group of other agents

to go with him. Bernie watched as they ran over to a beat-up green trash bin in the corner. At first, Bernie wondered why. But then, after Sharpears entered a secret access code hidden near the bottom of it, a door swung open. Bernie's eyes widened when she saw that the inside of the bin was sparkling clean and loaded with all kinds of tech.

"Wow, that's clever!" said Bernie.

"We have EEKs all over the city. They're available for all agents to use."

"Why is it called an EEK?" asked Jarvis.

"It stands for Emergency Equipment Krate. EEK. Your goggles should show you where the nearest one is and will display the access code. The codes are updated on a daily basis."

"Nice!" said Jarvis enthusiastically. Bernie noted that anytime technology was mentioned, Jarvis would light up. She liked seeing him optimistic rather than worrying all the time.

Man, I hope I get a chance to peek inside that EEK, thought Bernie. She really wanted to get her paws on some of that high-tech equipment.

Major Flatpaw gave similar orders to the other agents in attendance. They were all instructed to use their Mouse Watch–issued goggles to record everything they saw, hoping to find any clue that would indicate exactly how the humans were being subdued and, if possible, to retrieve a spray dispenser.

Finally, the only agents who were left were Bernie and Jarvis. Major Flatpaw turned her severe gaze upon the new recruits. She softened a little as she observed how young and inexperienced they looked.

"And as for you two, I'm going to try to go easy on ya. All I really want from you is to keep a close eye on the Times Square subway entrance. If you see anything suspicious, report it over your goggles' transmitter." She sighed. "Whiskerpaw informed me that you haven't even made it to basic training yet and I don't want you to get hurt. We've reached out to Gadget and Chip and Dale and informed them about the situation, so hopefully you won't need to be in the field very long. Help yourself to anything in the EEK, but please, no weapons. Just surveillance and safety equipment." She gave them both a stern look and wagged her finger warningly as she added, "And by all means, stay put."

Bernie was about to say that she would be fine and to not worry, but before she could say anything, the major turned and marched away. She and Jarvis exchanged glances.

"Well, I guess we'll be getting our training directly in the field," said Bernie. "Isn't this exciting?"

"Not really," said Jarvis worriedly. "I kind of liked learning in a place where dying wasn't a possibility."

"You worry too much," said Bernie. "We're gonna be just fine. Nothing bad will happen, okay?"

In spite of her confidence, Bernie's words didn't make Jarvis feel any better. But as for Bernie, fear always snapped her into action. She practically danced in place with excitement. Her first mission!

Bernie led Jarvis over to the equipment "krate." After entering the code displayed on her goggles, they stepped inside the cool tech center. Bernie felt like she'd walked inside the greatest spy and surveillance toy store that she'd ever seen! Staring around at all the gadgets mounted on the walls, she could hardly decide on what items to choose.

"Wow, I need one of those. It looks like a hair clip but it's also a homing device." Grinning, she grabbed one and clipped it in her hair. "Oooh, and look at these!" Bernie said, holding up a pair of slipper socks.

"Socks?" asked Jarvis.

"Not socks," said Bernie. "PARA-SHOES! It's a compressed parachute that fits over your hind paws. Let's try them on!"

Bernie took one pair for herself and handed the other to Jarvis. They looked like slipper socks except they were made of some kind of really tough, tightly woven fabric. The soles of the slippers had treads on them that provided extra traction, and when Bernie put them on, they conformed to the exact shape of her paws.

She walked around in the trailer, noticing that her footsteps were suddenly muffled and nearly soundproof. She jumped and was surprised to see that when she landed, she didn't make a sound.

"Cool!" she said.

"Yeah," said Jarvis. "Makes sneaking around much easier." His eyes fell on a small gray box. It didn't look like much to Bernie, but she saw his eyes widen with amazement.

"That's impossible," he said.

"What is?" asked Bernie.

Jarvis held up the little box, examining it like he'd found a rare, priceless artifact.

"It says that it's a 10G wireless signal booster. Do you realize what that means for streaming content and download speeds?" he asked excitedly. "I mean, 10G? I had no idea that was even possible! I've always just stolen Wi-Fi from the humans I live with. Man, I could rocket to the top of the leaderboard in Mousecraft so fast with this, nobody would see it coming!"

"I have no idea what you're talking about," admitted Bernie. Then feeling like she should humor him, she added, "How fast is it?"

"The speed of lightning times two," said Jarvis. He

stared down at the little oblong box longingly. "Do you think it would be okay if we took one?"

"Major Flatpaw said to help ourselves as long as it's not a weapon, so I don't see why not," said Bernie. Jarvis let out a squeak of excitement. Bernie laughed.

Bernie and Jarvis loaded up their pockets with several interesting items that might come in handy, including a pocket-size Drone Summoner, which would locate the nearest self-driving Mouse Watch drone and bring it directly to them. Jarvis took some climbing pegs that were inside a bandolier he could wear over his shoulder. Bernie noticed that they had once been simple foam-rubber darts with suction tips that were usually used in human children's Nerf guns, but had been modified for extra "stickability."

They knew they were only supposed to wait by the subway entrance and probably wouldn't get to use any of this stuff, but just holding it was exciting.

With bulging pockets, she and Jarvis stuck to the shadows as they scampered over to the closest subway entrance, taking positions on either side of a fire hydrant. Bernie scanned the area with her goggles, noting the descriptions of the various rats milling about on the streets that were depicted in pop-up tags on her view screen.

"Well, most of them don't have any suspicious items on them," said Bernie after studying the descriptions on her display window.

"Wait a second," said Jarvis, squinting through his goggles. "What's going on with that guy over there?"

Bernie followed the direction in which he was pointing. A rat wearing a lab coat with the number sixteen on the pocket was standing in an alleyway and talking to himself. She told the goggles to magnify the image by thirty percent so she could confirm what she was seeing.

"Who's he talking to?" asked Bernie.

"Beats me," admitted Jarvis. "But let me try to see if there's any kind of Bluetooth signal."

Reaching into his pocket, he removed a mini-microphone and plugged it into the side of his goggles.

"I should have grabbed one of those when we were at the EEK," Bernie said enviously. "Where were they?"

"By the smoke-screen pellets," said Jarvis. He adjusted a small knob on the side of the goggles and listened intently. "Yep, he's talking to someone on some kind of Bluetooth earpiece. I think it's a private channel because my goggles don't register the network that it's on at all." He tilted his big, round ear forward and listened some more. "Whoever it is he's talking to, they have a voice like a rusted hinge."

Jarvis stared intently at the figure across the street as he listened. "He said a name. I think he said . . . Doctor . . . Corncob."

"Dr. Corncob?" asked Bernie. "That doesn't sound right. Are you sure you're not just hungry?"

"No wait, hang on. . . . It's Thornpaw. Dr. Thornpaw."

"Now THAT sounds more like a rat name," said Bernie. She rolled her eyes and mumbled, "Corncob, seriously?"

"Mmm, corn," said Jarvis, licking his lips. "A little Tabasco on some hot, buttered corn. That would be so good right now. . . ."

"He's moving!" whispered Bernie. "Let's follow him! Stay low!" And before Jarvis could say otherwise, Bernie shot off after the mysterious rat.

"Why does she always do that?" he muttered. Then, as he loped after her, he added worriedly, "I just know we're going to get in trouble for this."

Number Sixteen half ran, half walked out of the alley and down the sidewalk. Bernie and Jarvis were close behind, but they made sure to stick to every wall, stoop, and gutter as they followed. Sixteen made a left at a Greek bistro packed with rat customers. Then he made a quick right, jumped onto the stairs of a nearby city bus, and squeezed through a tiny crack between the folding doors.

"Should we follow him?" asked Jarvis.

"Let's see if he comes back out first," said Bernie.

The two crouched behind a soda can that had fallen on the floor near one of the tables. After about thirty seconds, Bernie felt concerned.

"All right, something's up," she said. "We need to get over there and find out where he went."

But just as they were about to leave their hiding place, the hydraulic doors of the bus sprang open. The wafting, delicious smell of melted cheese filled the air as a dozen glassy-eyed humans stepped down the stairs. Number Sixteen was right behind them, along with a second rat. Bernie noticed that this one had a number twenty-eight on its pocket and that it carried a large device on its shoulders. It had a clear tank filled with orange liquid and a spray nozzle. A big troop of rats with variously numbered lab coats followed behind Number Twenty-eight. The last rat, a hulking female with the number sixty-six on her coat, carried a second sprayer. This one, Bernie noticed, was filled with purple liquid. It was a particular shade of sparkling lavender that she felt she recognized from somewhere. It took her a second, but then she had it. She knew that color! It was the same unique color of the mist from the drone that had released sleeping gas on everyone in LA's Union Station.

It was Gadget's memory-erasing Sleep Spray.

Bernie put two and two together. It was too coincidental. Somehow the rats had gotten their hands on Gadget's formula and were using it, *altering* it to affect the humans.

"Did you see that?" hissed Bernie excitedly. "Those are the sprayers that Whiskerpaw told us about. We've got to get the orange one with the cheese scent. The purple is filled with Gadget's Sleep Spray."

"Well, good luck with that," said Jarvis. "There's rats everywhere. If they spot us, we're done for."

The two watched as the zombie humans were led to the nearest subway station stairs and, like orderly ants, continued down below. None of them seemed to have the least idea of where they were or what was happening.

"Come on," said Bernie.

"Wait!" squeaked Jarvis. "Just wait a second. Maybe we should just report this back to HQ and not get too close to the danger. I don't see any version of following all those rats down there where we wouldn't get hurt."

Bernie leveled a stare at him. "Jarvis. Agents get hurt sometimes. That's what we signed up for."

"I know, but . . . you heard Flatpaw. We don't have any training. We're just supposed to stay put."

"No buts! The only 'butt' should be yours following mine after those rats. We gotta help those humans and get that sprayer. We can report back when we bring it with us. Can you imagine how relieved everyone will be if we actually get that thing? We can save lives!"

Jarvis looked conflicted, and Bernie could tell how scared he was. But his expression told her that he knew Bernie was right. Being a Mouse Watch agent sometimes meant taking risks.

"Let's go," said Bernie.

Jarvis reluctantly nodded. He removed several of the

Nerf darts from his bandolier, handed two of them to Bernie, and kept two for himself.

"We can be smart about this," he said firmly. "Let's stick to the walls and not get spotted."

And by "sticking to the walls" Bernie soon realized that Jarvis meant it literally. As soon as they got to the stairs, Jarvis stuck one of the dart's suction cups to the tiled wall and then, after plopping it in place, he stabbed a second one next to it, creating handholds.

The rat worked hand over hand, sticking them one at a time. Right hand, stick. Left hand, stick. Right hand, stick. Left hand, stick. As he worked, he swung back and forth, creating each handhold as he held himself suspended high above the stairs and the platform below where the rats were gathered, staying out of their range of vision. It was impressive to watch. Maybe she had underestimated her partner after all.

"Okay, here goes," Bernie said to herself, and followed him.

CHAPTER 17

Bernie's arms burned with exertion from climbing, but she held on tight, knowing that to fall now would mean certain death. Her arms shook a little as she gazed at the scene below, taking in what the goggles revealed to her about the people involved.

A pop-up balloon identified the numerous rats, the Mouse Watch database informing Bernie if there were any known criminals among them. Most of the rats must have been recently recruited because they had no case files available. There were, however, a couple of notable exceptions.

Germy Fangtooth, armed robbery. Assault.

Bernie read the rap sheet associated with the piebald rat, noting that he was considered "armed and dangerous."

Better watch out for that one, she thought. He was

carrying one of the sprayer tanks with the orange mind-control formula inside of it.

The other exception was a rat named Tiny Leathertoes. Contrary to his name, he was the biggest rat Bernie had ever seen! He hulked over the other rats and nearly came up to a human's knee. His prison record was even more extensive than Fangtooth's and included some terribly violent acts that Bernie really wished she hadn't found out about.

Hopefully he's slow. Speed is going to be our best chance of getting in and out of here alive.

"So, what do we do now?" asked Jarvis as they clung to their foam darts, high above the rats and out of sight.

"Hang on, I'm thinking," said Bernie.

"We have to do something," said Jarvis.

The truth was, Bernie realized, they were kind of winging it. Without any special training for handling a hostage situation, she really had no idea of what she was supposed to do.

"What are they doing?" Jarvis asked worriedly.

Bernie noticed that the rats were ushering the humans down a small ladder that led from the platform to the tracks below. Once a human was there, Tiny Leathertoes would position them directly on the track, facing toward the empty tunnel. The rats continued lining them up, one by one, and Bernie noticed that the expression on the two criminal rats' faces was one of sinister anticipation, as if something terrible was coming and they couldn't wait to see it happen.

Bernie suddenly realized what they were up to and shuddered so violently, she almost lost her grip on the darts she was holding.

"They're gonna run them down!" she whispered.

"Wait. What?" squeaked Jarvis.

"The humans! They're—"

But her whisper was cut off by the long, low blast of a subway train's horn. Somewhere down the tunnel was a train—probably piloted by rats. And Bernie had a feeling they wouldn't be hitting the brakes.

"We gotta get down there, quick!" she said.

"Bernie, have you seen us? How are we going to stop a train that size?" exclaimed Jarvis.

"I have an idea. When we drop down there, you cause a distraction."

"Me?" Jarvis looked pale. "What kind of distraction?"

"I don't know, think of something . . . distracting. While everyone's attention is focused on you, I'll get the humans off the tracks."

"Focused on *me*?" Jarvis whispered.

"Yeah. While hundreds of eyes are looking at you, I'll grab the purple sprayer and put all the rats to sleep. Maybe I can take down their leader, too, and demand he tell us what happened to the LA agents. After that, we'll make them take us to Dr. Thornpaw."

Jarvis looked at her with a mix of awe and doubt. "Bernie, you're a really brave mouse. But you have no training! How are you going to do all that?"

Bernie set her face in a determined expression. "I have to try, don't I?"

The train horn bellowed again, getting closer.

"We gotta move! How do we get down?" said Bernie.

"Para-shoes," said Jarvis. Bernie was glad he thought so quickly on his feet. It must have been his famous puzzle-solving skills.

"Right!" said Bernie. She'd forgotten she'd put them on back at the EEK. She looked down at her feet with her goggles and was happy to see a pop-up balloon appear with instructions on how to use the Para-shoes.

Click heels twice and leap free of all obstacles.

"Okay, I'm going. Click your heels twice and jump!" said Bernie.

After taking a quick breath, Bernie clicked her heels twice and released her hands from the Nerf darts on the wall. She jumped as far out as she could. Jarvis, not wanting to be left behind, followed quickly after.

They'd barely cleared the wall when the Para-shoes deployed their chutes. They worked perfectly—well, almost perfectly. Bernie hadn't considered that because they were on her feet, the Para-shoes swooped them both upside down. As she and Jarvis were drifting upside down toward Earth, she couldn't help letting out a surprised squeal!

They were able to land gently, paws-first on the ground. But Bernie's squeal had caused all the rats to stop what they were doing and glance over in their direction. Bernie and Jarvis froze. All eyes were on them.

It certainly was the distraction Bernie had asked for. But, unfortunately, all the attention was on her, too.

Germy Fangtooth turned from the human he'd just led to the tracks. A confused look crossed his ugly, crumpled face.

"Jarvis Slinktail?"

Bernie gave Jarvis a sharp look. How did this notorious R.A.T.S. criminal know him by name?

Jarvis, thinking quickly, removed a small device from his pocket and fired it at the rat. A condensed cloud of Gadget's purple sleeping spray surrounded Germy, who promptly fell asleep.

"Why didn't you tell me you had that?" demanded Bernie.

"I forgot until now! I grabbed one of these Mini Sleepers just before we left the EEK. I thought it might come in handy."

Conveniently handy, mused Bernie. *Especially when you've just been recognized by the enemy and you want to shut him up*.

A horn blasted. Bernie looked into the dark tunnel, past the row of stupefied humans, and saw the distant headlight of an approaching train. There was no time left!

Suddenly, a chorus of shouts saying "FOR THE WATCH!" rang out from the stairway that led to the street above. Bernie wheeled around, and what she saw made her heart leap for joy. A group of Mouse Watch agents charged down the stairs with their weapons drawn.

Bernie knew she had to take advantage of the distraction. While all the rats rushed to meet the advancing agents, Bernie had only one goal . . . to save the humans! The train was seconds away. How in the world could she get them off the tracks in time?

Desperate for a solution, she rummaged through her pockets. As luck would have it, her paw seized upon the one gadget that could help her now.

SUP-A DUP-A INST-A GLUE-A. BONDS WITH ANYTHING SO FAST YOU WON'T BELIEVE IT. STRONG ENOUGH TO EASILY HOLD FIFTY TONS.

When she'd grabbed it back at the EEK, she'd done so because she thought it might come in handy if she ever broke something by accident—like a window, or one of her bones. If she'd had it back when she'd done the zip line with Poopie, she might have been able to glue her parents' smartphone back together. But now, gazing at the incoming train, she knew she had only a few seconds to spare if she were to do the thing she had in mind.

Bernie leaped through the crowd of fighting rats and agents. Because she was so small, most of them didn't see her as she dodged and wove among the tangle of furry fighting bodies. The headlight of the train was coming out of the tunnel now. The human in front, a little girl, stared straight at it with a frozen expression. Bernie saw the bright light reflected in her lifeless stare. A word escaped her lips, the merest whisper, "Smells so . . . cheesy. . . . "

With a mighty leap, Bernie sprang from the subway platform. For a second she flew through the air before landing perfectly on the track below. She ran nimbly along the biggest rail as fast as she possibly could, speeding toward the incoming train. She was so close she could feel the vibrations through her whiskers.

When she was just a few feet from the humans, she unstoppered the glue and squeezed it all over the grimy metal tracks. Sharp, pungent fumes filled her nostrils as the glue made contact with the metal. The tracks shook as the train sped closer. Bernie looked up just in time to see the huge wheels screaming toward her.

At the last possible moment, she dove out of the way, closing her eyes. There was a tremendous SCREECH, as if all the metal in the world were suddenly scraping and bending at once. A mouse's heart can beat 632 times per minute, but Bernie's felt like it was beating twice that fast!

When the sound stopped, Bernie looked up to see that the train had stopped just a few feet from the humans. The rats in the conductor's seat had been thrown through the windows and were all piled in a heap, staring stupidly around them as if they were unable to comprehend what had just happened.

"YES!" Bernie pumped her fist in the air.

Suddenly, she felt a strong paw grip her shoulder. Fearing an attack, Bernie wheeled around and put her paws up in a pose she'd seen the Watchers practicing back at HQ during her tour.

"Agent Skampersky! You need to come with us!" Major Flatpaw's glowing blue goggles stared down at her.

"Major! Did you get the sprayer?" she asked breathlessly. "Where's Jarvis? Is he okay?"

"We've got it. The rats are taken care of for now, but you know the saying about rats: If you see one, there are more nearby. Jarvis is up on the platform with the rest of the agents. We've got to go now! Here, take this!"

The agent handed Bernie a white tube with a glowing blue button.

"What do I do with this?" she asked.

The major produced one for herself. "It's called a Pop! Cycle." She pressed the button, and the tube popped open. Within the blink of an eye, nanobots had assembled the sleekest-looking mouse-size motorcycle Bernie had ever seen!

"Okay, let's move out!" shouted Flatpaw.

"Wait!" said Bernie. She glanced over to the stunned rats that had been thrown from the train and spotted one that was unconscious. Dashing over, she located a silver device in his ear and yanked it out.

"Here," said Bernie.

"What is it?" asked Major Flatpaw.

"It's a communication device. They're using it to talk to someone called Dr. Thornpaw. He seems to be giving them all orders."

"Good work, Skampersky. The director will definitely want a look at this. Maybe we can use it to trace back the source of the signal."

Bernie beamed. But she didn't have time to revel in the compliment. Flatpaw mounted her Pop! Cycle, lowered her goggles, and gunned the engine. She called back to Bernie as she rocketed off, "Mount up!"

Bernie didn't have to be told twice. Even though she'd never ridden a motorcycle before, she followed the agent's lead, leaping onto her Pop! Cycle and slamming her finger on the START button.

She'd wanted a motorcycle for a long, long time. And now she had one.

VARRR-OOOM!

The Pop! Cycle let out an electronic roar. Bernie had no time to react as the bike shot forward, racing alongside the train tracks faster than the train itself. She careened up a maintenance ramp, following the agent in front. Back on the high platform, she saw what the major had been talking about: Almost all of the rats had been immobilized in heavy, collapsible nets. But there were also a few big ones running free, wielding pocketknives, which, although small for humans, made deadly swords in the hands of a rodent. Racing along, she spotted Jarvis with the other agents. Now that the sprayer was in hand, they were preparing to evacuate.

Bernie saw an agent toss Jarvis a Pop! Cycle tube, but Jarvis immediately let it slip through his fingers. The important piece of tech clattered to the floor and rolled over to the feet of an approaching rat.

"No!" Jarvis dove to save it, but the rat brandished a pocketknife in his direction. Jarvis took one look at the thug and dashed away through the crowd.

Bernie's suspicions resurfaced. What if Jarvis was just pretending that he was afraid of the R.A.T.S. but was secretly working as a double agent? Dropping an important piece of technology at their feet might be one way to work with them without making it *look* like he was in league with them. She just couldn't shake the memory of the rat that had recognized him earlier, and it really bothered her.

Better keep my friends close and my enemies closer, she thought. *When we get back to HQ I'll tell the director all about it. If he thinks Jarvis might be the spy, then we'll have him in custody.*

"Jarvis! Over here!"

Bernie raced her cycle to Jarvis and grabbed him, helping him jump onto the back. She joined the group of agents on motorcycles as a roar from a side tunnel filled the station. Glancing back over her shoulder, she saw the unmistakable shapes of a fleet of Mouse Watch drones from Los Angeles HQ hurtling forward. Her heart soared. Surely they were piloted by the Mouse Watch agents who had gone missing—Alph and Digit and the rest of the California team. The thought was almost enough to distract her from the hordes of R.A.T.S. agents pouring out of the side tunnel.

But Bernie's spirits sank when she realized the rats were cheering the drones on, roaring in approval as they chased down the fleeing Watchers.

"They have our drones!" Bernie shouted. She twisted the throttle on the handle of her cycle and shot off after the agents, racing back up the subway stairs and onto the city streets above. *Gotta get back to base, we're outnumbered!*

The mice on bikes roared through the rat-infested streets like a wild, high-tech motorcycle gang. The Watchers' gleaming bikes responded to the slightest touch, maneuvering easily between any obstacles in their path. As the drones closed in, several of the agents broke ranks, peeling off down side streets to try to shake their pursuers.

Bernie had never ridden a motorcycle before and was surprised that her slightest touch sent the bike wobbling this way and that, swerving between parked cars and narrowly missing a row of parking meters.

"AAAAAAGH!" she screamed as she and Jarvis ducked their heads at the last minute, just missing a gigantic pigeon that could have knocked them right off the bike.

"Watch out!" shouted Jarvis, pointing at the wheel of a taxi that Bernie only managed to avoid at the last possible second. "Stop swerving so much!"

"I can't help it!"

Gotta get control of this thing! Bernie thought. And no sooner had she thought it than something exploded behind her, and a foul stench enveloped her and Jarvis. It was so overpowering that Bernie almost lost control of her bike, swerved, then regained control just before crashing into a hot-dog cart.

"What *is* that?" she yelled.

"It smells like . . . like . . . *stinky cheese bombs*!" Jarvis moaned.

As Bernie wiped smelly, melty Limburger cheese from her fur, she caught a glimpse of the pilot, a leering rat with a scar down her nose, laughing maniacally as she went buzzing by. Leave it to rats to turn something delicious into a weapon.

Miraculously, Bernie managed to hang on and control the bike. She zipped over a rain gutter, navigating along one of the metal slats like on a tightrope to avoid falling through. She let out a triumphant shout as the bike raced away with the R.A.T.S. hot on her and Jarvis's heels. "WHOOHOOOOO!" she yelled as the wind whipped through her fur.

This is what Bernie had always dreamed being a Mouse Watch agent would be like.

Well, except for being covered in cheese that smelled like feet.

CHAPTER 18

The farther Bernie rode the Pop! Cycle, the better she got at it. She was a natural. With the drones hot on her tail, she had to reach deep and focus her instincts for survival. She tore through the streets of New York, doing everything possible to shake her pursuers.

At a certain point, Bernie realized the rest of the agents were nowhere to be found—they had all swerved off in different directions.

"How many drones are behind us?" Bernie shouted over her shoulder.

Jarvis hazarded a look. "There's three," he shouted back. "And it looks like they're gaining on us."

"Hang on!" shouted Bernie as she twisted the throttle and sped down a side street. She swerved underneath abandoned buses and taxis that loomed above them like mountains, used stray litter such as tin cans as ramps onto the high curb, and navigated through sidewalks. Since most of the humans were underground, there was no need to worry about being stepped on.

She saw a sign for Bowling Green on her right. Bernie, being a native of California, had no idea where in New York that was, but when she spotted the big park and the many trees, she made a split-second decision. She made a quick turn into the park, where the grass under her wheels made her feel as if she were off-roading. Fortunately, Gadget had seen to it that the motorcycles could handle almost any terrain. Bernie pushed through grass taller than her head and made sure to swerve around every massive tree trunk she could find.

The maneuver worked beautifully. *THUD! THUD! THUD!* The sound of drones smacking into the overhead branches behind them made Bernie and Jarvis cheer.

"You got 'em!" shouted Jarvis excitedly as he watched two of the drones get caught in the tree branches and the third smash directly into the trunk of a huge maple and erupt into an explosion of cheese and flames.

Bernie sped through Bowling Green Park and past a sign that said BATTERY PARK. There, she skidded to a stop, breathing hard. As she paused to catch her breath, she glanced back at Jarvis. The rat was white as a sheet but looked as relieved as she felt. Suddenly, the two of them grinned at each other and burst out laughing.

"Okay," Bernie said. "You have to admit that was fun."

"It was fun." Jarvis smiled. "When it was over."

Bernie glanced down at the motorcycle with a growing feeling of love and admiration. It wasn't the way she'd dreamed of learning to ride one, but it had worked. She patted the frame of the bike affectionately.

"I guess that agent back at New York HQ, Cooper, was right. *There's no better teacher than firsthand experience.*"

Bernie was about to turn around and head back to Mouse Watch HQ when her whiskers twitched like radar. She picked up the scent of something suspicious.

"Hey," she said to Jarvis. "I smell something weird."

"Uh, Bernie? I think it's us." They both still had the remains of the stinky cheese bomb stuck in their fur.

"No, that's not it." She turned in a circle, then pulled Jarvis behind a big tree. "Look over there!"

They peeked out. On the other side of the park was the Hudson River. A big boat was docked in the harbor, under a sign that said FERRY TO STATUE OF LIBERTY.

"A big boat?" said Jarvis. "I don't know, water freaks me out."

"No," said Bernie. "Down there." She shifted Jarvis's gaze to the loading dock, where a group of small shadows was squeezing through a vent in the bottom of the boat. "What's that? Oh, great . . . rats," Jarvis said with a grimace.

Excitement swelled inside of her. "Do you know what this means?"

"No," confessed Jarvis.

"The Statue of Liberty. Why would rats take a boat to the Statue of Liberty unless . . ."

"That's where Corncob—er, *Thornpaw* is!"

Bernie wheeled around excitedly and grabbed Jarvis by his shoulders. "We have to follow them. This might be our chance to take him down!"

"I don't know," said Jarvis. "We promised to meet back at HQ. We can't take on Thornpaw alone. We need backup."

Bernie's excitement was quickly replaced with suspicion. She released his shoulders and crossed her arms. "Interesting," she said flatly.

"What do you mean?" asked Jarvis.

"Oh, I just think it's interesting that now that we're close to getting the villain behind all this, you don't want to go. It's like you *want* them to get away. I also think it's interesting that you conveniently dropped your Pop! Cycle back there at the subway for the R.A.T.S. to find."

"Wait. Are you accusing me AGAIN?" said Jarvis, his long whiskers vibrating in frustration. "I dropped that Pop! Cycle by accident. And just because I don't want to rush in without a plan and get killed doesn't mean I'm a traitor or a spy!" Jarvis looked really hurt and angry. "Every time I try, you keep shutting me down. You judge me. You always assume the worst. Fine, if you want to go and get the bad guy all by yourself, you go right ahead. I don't even care anymore."

"Fine, I will!" retorted Bernie. "And after I get him, I'm going to tell Director Whiskerpaw about all I've seen. I'll let him decide what to do with you."

"Fine!"

"Fine!"

Jarvis stalked off through the tall grass. Bernie swatted her tail on the ground in anger. Then she mounted the Pop! Cycle, lowered her goggles, and took off for the ferry. She was boiling mad and more determined than ever to prove that she was right. Right about Jarvis and right about following her guts. Right that she deserved a place in the Mouse Watch.

When she was within hearing distance of the ferry, she dismounted the bike, pressed the blue button, and watched in admiration as it folded itself back into a sleek white tube. Bernie shoved it in the pocket of her jumpsuit and scampered as quietly as she could to the dock, hiding behind a tall buoy. The last of the rats were climbing into the vent.

"What are you doing???" a small voice whispered urgently. Bernie turned around and saw a mouse family hiding underneath a red life preserver that was propped up against a fence. There was a father, a mother, and a baby mouse huddling alongside what looked a lot like a suitcase from the Winter Nancy collection.

"Don't *follow* them!" the mother cried. "You should be hiding, like the rest of us." Bernie's heart cried out to the baby and her parents, the little family forced into hiding. The last rat was climbing into the ferry, and the horn blew.

"I'll be back," Bernie said. "I'll make it safe again. I'm in the Mouse Watch. That's my job." Then she scampered as fast as she could to the boat and dove through a different vent just as it was pulling away.

And as she felt the water beneath the boat surge by and the towering symbol of liberty grow ever closer, she was determined not to let anyone underestimate who she was and what she was capable of.

She would find this Dr. Thornpaw.

And she would bring him to justice.

As she congratulated herself on her sneakiness and raw courage, she didn't see the long shadow grow closer and closer behind her. Then, without any warning, something heavy hit her in the back of the head, and the world as she knew it faded quickly away.

CHAPTER 19

Bernie awoke stiff with pain.

Her arm hurt.

Her ribs hurt.

And her head felt like it was about to explode.

As she gazed around herself, at first she thought she'd gone blind. The entire world was a featureless white. But as she rose shakily to her feet, she realized with a sigh of relief that she was wrong. She was just surrounded by very high white walls.

A voice, a horrible one, sounded from somewhere above her. Tilting her head toward the ceiling, she saw, suspended on a platform, a monstrous creature. He had once been a rat, it seemed, but now he was . . . something else. Almost all of his limbs had been replaced by metal appendages, and the parts of his body that hadn't been replaced were singed and scarred.

"Welcome to my laboratory, one of the most prime pieces of real estate in New York. Liberty's crown! I would imagine that you never thought you'd find yourself here and that it would look like this." The figure gestured with a metal claw.

Now that she could see who was speaking, the reality of Dr. Thornpaw's identity was far more horrible than she ever could have imagined. It took a moment, but Bernie realized that she had seen him before.

"You!" she said.

Dr. Thornpaw chuckled.

"Yes, I remember you, Bernie Skampersky. You were the tiny mouse who tried to chase me after I killed your brother. It made me laugh for days. Left a big impression."

"Come down here and fight!" screamed Bernie. She was filled with a white-hot rage like she'd never felt before. All the fur on her body stood on end. She was so close to the creature that had taken her brother from her, so close to finally getting revenge for the pain and hurt he'd caused her and her parents.

"Now, now, calm down," cooed Dr. Thornpaw. "You have a unique opportunity here, and I'd like to see old grudges put aside in favor of a more intelligent path." Thornpaw grinned, exposing his yellowed, broken teeth. Bernie cringed as the doctor continued, saying, "The truth is, I could use someone like you. Someone with determination and grit. Someone who isn't afraid to break the rules. You and I are more similar than you think."

Bernie felt a wave of revulsion at the doctor's words. "I'm nothing like you," she retorted.

"Oh, but you are," croaked the doctor with a smile. "I overheard the way you spoke with Jarvis. The earpieces that my lab rats use have a much wider range than you would ever believe. And I was impressed with your judgment."

"What do you mean, 'my judgment'?" snarled Bernie.

"You judged him quite well, I think," said Dr. Thornpaw. "He is an inferior breed of rat. He abandoned a chance at achieving greatness to join a hopeless cause with the Mouse Watch. It all comes down to evolution, the survival of the fittest. You made it quite clear that you were suspicious of his motives and that you didn't trust him in spite of his protestations that he's been nothing but loyal. I like that quality in someone who works for me. Trust is for fools."

Bernie's mind reeled. She hadn't judged Jarvis so harshly, had she? She hated the way Thornpaw was trying to manipulate her thinking.

"Jarvis is a traitor," she said. "All evidence points to that."

The doctor nodded eagerly. "Yes, yes he is. He betrayed me, too! See? Once again, we agree! I'll bet we agree on all kinds of things, like what it is to be misjudged because of our appearance or to feel victimized by lesser beings who don't see our potential."

Bernie's cheeks flushed with shame. How often had she felt those things? To think that Thornpaw felt the same made her feel gross. There was a little truth in his words and that made them all the more unpleasant to hear.

Seeing her hesitate, Dr. Thornpaw pressed his advantage.

"I'm going to make you a job offer. I see a lot of myself in you and I don't want to see you go down a path that will limit your potential. If you'll join me, I'll train you with the R.A.T.S. We accept all kinds of critters here—rats, mice, lizards, hamsters, the occasional spirited guinea pig. You're still young and impressionable. I'm offering you a chance at the greatness you know you deserve."

Bernie gritted her teeth with suppressed anger. She'd believed in the Mouse Watch ever since she could remember. And now her sworn enemy, the one that she'd built her life on finding and bringing to justice, was trying to get her to turn on them. She'd never expected that, not in a million years.

Secretly, she was ashamed of herself. Dr. Thornpaw admitted that Jarvis was a traitor to *him*. That her new partner had betrayed R.A.T.S. to come and fight on the side of good. To Bernie, that said everything she needed to know about his noble character. Jarvis had been right and Bernie had been wrong. And now that she was in the doctor's clutches, she might never have a chance to apologize.

"I'll never join you," she growled (or as much of a growl as a mouse her size could muster). "I'd rather die."

Dr. Thornpaw shrugged, looking disappointed.

"Oh, but I have a feeling you will," croaked the doctor. "Do you see those walls around you? From my vantage point up here, they rather resemble a maze—and a tricky one at that. In fact, the maze in which you find yourself is quite dangerous. It is both like, and unlike, the types humans have been using on rodents for many years."

Bernie gritted her teeth and stayed silent.

"I was required to run a similar maze when I was trapped by human scientists many years ago. Subjected to many cruel experiments, tests that left me as you see me now. Research, they called it."

The doctor began to pace, thinking aloud to himself. "I have, of course, made the best of a bad situation. However, as you recently discovered, I wasn't going to let the wrongs done to me go unpunished."

Thornpaw raised a metal finger and continued, saying, "Under the influence of my cheese spray, the humans will experience everything that was done to me and more. Also, as is my policy, any rodent that resists my efforts will be subjected to similar ordeals."

The doctor turned his single bloodshot eye upon Bernie.

"You may have captured my sprayer, which is, admittedly, a crude but effective device. However, once the drones are filled with my formula, I assure you that it will take very little time to subjugate the masses on a much grander scale than I was capable of before. So, with a R.A.T.S. victory now within my grasp, I will observe and document all the data that my experiments reveal. In other words, your body and mind will be sacrificed for the sake of science."

Bernie was about to speak when the doctor held up a finger. "I want to introduce you to someone who was wiser than yourself. Someone who I hope you'll think about as you remember the decision you made not to join me. He has proven himself loyal and has earned my trust and the rewards that go with it."

The doctor motioned and a figure joined him on the balcony. Bernie was surprised to see Agent Cooper, the tired old mouse with baggy eyes that she'd briefly met at the New York office. But then, a second later, his image shimmered. A new mouse was standing there, a mouse Bernie could hardly believe she was looking at.

"Digit?" she said.

"Hello, Bernie," said the graying agent with a smirk.

"It was you? You were the spy?" she said.

"Been doing it for years." He tapped the side of his goggles and grinned. "Disguising myself as Cooper, I got all the info I needed in New York to pass along to the good doctor here. Meanwhile, in LA they never expected a thing, never thought old Digit would betray them. It was so easy! Plus, I have to say, the doctor here knows how to reward those who help him. He's a great boss and has a wonderful pension plan. Imagine, all the cheese you could ever want for the rest of your life! Totally worth it."

A renewed feeling of guilt and shame washed over her for thinking that Jarvis was the spy—and all because he was different from her. She'd been so unfair. If she'd just been more accepting, maybe they could have been friends—Bernie's first true friend. But it was too late now.

Bernie glared up at Digit and Dr. Thornpaw. Her tail went stiff and her face was red with rage. "You're a traitor and he's a monster!"

"A monster, you say?" said Thornpaw.

The doctor's eye narrowed and his grimace twisted upward in something between a sneer and a smile. He held up a steel claw and said, "See this? I crafted this *enhancement* after some scientists wanted to find out what would happen to the nerves in my paw if it was exposed to an acid-based cleaning product." He pointed at his artificial eye. "And this . . . oh, I gave this little *gift* to myself after they wanted to see what would happen if a new chemically bonding lipstick happened to get in someone's eye. That little experiment hurt quite a bit, I can tell you."

Thornpaw gestured at his mechanical legs. "And these were my greatest achievements. After gathering data on what happens to a rat's legs if they're subjected to electric shocks for a year, they discovered that they atrophy. Big surprise! However, I've made the best of that little blunder, too."

Thornpaw raised himself up to full height and snarled, "I know what it is to have physical shortcomings. I have overcome them all and am more powerful and better than before. I'll never forgive them for what they did to me and yet, I'm also grateful. It has enabled me to exact revenge and usher in an entirely new world, one where they will feel the same kind of pain I did. You are a small-minded and small-bodied rodent. Digit told me that you had potential, but you disappoint me, Bernie Skampersky."

Bernie hardly knew what to say. Thornpaw was so worked up that little bits of foam and spittle hovered around his twisted mouth. His eye was filled with manic energy, fueled by hate.

He gazed down at her and said, "And therefore, you're about to be educated. You will soon be shaped by pain, too. It will be a chance for you to overcome your physical deformity. You'll be tested. And, after spending years as an experimental study, you might change your mind about which side you are on," said the doctor. "If after learning your lesson you decide to join me, perhaps I can do something about that tiny bone structure . . . give you an upgrade."

Bernie had never felt so insulted or angry. But instead of firing back at Thornpaw, she instead glared at Digit and said, "What happened to Alph? You got her captured, didn't you?"

Digit shrugged. "Of course. Along with the entire Mouse Watch in Los Angeles. Alph's a good kid but terribly misguided. Like you, she bought into the whole philosophy of the Watch instead of realizing the truth. . . ." Digit leaned over the balcony and said with a cruel grin, "The fact is, there's nobody more important than yourself. Nature demands the survival of the fittest. You have to take care of number one. Everything about the Watch being as good as all of its parts is sentimental nonsense. In the end, it's every mouse for itself."

And Bernie realized at that moment exactly why it was so important to work as a team. She needed the wisdom of those around her to keep her informed and centered. She needed a partner like Jarvis, who had been so patient and kind and had faith in her. The reasons they had each been chosen by the Mouse Watch were different—but equally important. They could learn from each other. She also needed Gadget, an older, wiser mouse who could offer her guidance. She even needed Alph—a strong mouse who knew who she was. Alph was someone Bernie would be proud to call a friend, if she had the chance.

She saw where the other path led as she stared up at

these two pathetic rodents, each of whom was lost in his own arrogance. Being selfish and consumed with their own destiny had left them as empty husks inside.

They'd given up everything for power.

But in that moment, Bernie realized a very important truth: Life is about relationships with others.

And she also realized how misguided she'd been, trying to prove her own importance. Maybe that's why the doctor had thought he could sway her to the R.A.T.S. side.

Well, she knew better now.

If she ever got a second chance, she'd show the Watch that she knew how to stick together. She would be there for Jarvis, too . . . if he could ever forgive her.

"You know my answer," said Bernie quietly. "Do whatever you're going to do and be done with it."

Digit shook his head scornfully, mocking Bernie as if to say that she'd missed out on the most obvious of great opportunities.

The doctor's face showed no expression at all, but he seemed equally pleased by the prospect of having a new subject to experiment upon as an underling to obey his commands.

"Right. Well, then the task before you really is quite simple," he said.

The doctor gestured broadly. "From where I stand, I

can see the entirety of the maze. You, of course, can only see a few feet in front of you. Escape the maze and you'll go free. Fair enough?"

Bernie didn't believe she'd "go free" any more than she believed that Dr. Thornpaw could win a beauty contest. However, she nodded in response.

"How long do I have?" she asked.

"Why, as long as it takes!" replied the doctor. "You'll either starve or find sustenance, kill or be killed. For I assure you, this isn't simply a child's maze to be solved with paper and a pencil."

The doctor snapped his left claw, slamming it shut with a loud *CLANK!* Then he added, "The dangers that lurk inside of it will test your intelligence to its limits. I'm very much looking forward to seeing how long you survive, Bernie Skampersky."

Seeing the doctor's claw snap shut reminded her of something. Bernie had a flash of inspiration. She reached up to her hair and removed the homing beacon hair clip she'd retrieved from the EEK. When it was hidden in her hand, she pressed the tiny button that activated it. Then she called up to the doctor.

"Well, if you want to see what I'm capable of, I don't want anything to spoil the experiment. I shouldn't have any advantages except for my intellect, correct?"

The doctor raised his eyebrows. "That's correct. I need this to be a closed experiment in order to have data that's not corrupted."

"Then you should take this." She held up the hair clip. "It's a piece of Mouse Watch technology. It would help me navigate the maze and avoid all the obstacles. I don't need it to prove myself. I'm better than that."

The doctor studied her for a moment. "Do you think I'm an idiot? You're probably carrying an explosive!"

Bernie shook her head. "As an untrained agent I'm not allowed to carry a weapon."

Digit agreed, saying, "She's right. They wouldn't allow her to carry anything lethal."

The doctor motioned for a lab rat to lower a small container, Bernie placed the hair clip inside, and he pulled it back up. When he'd retrieved it, he examined it carefully, noting the tiny power light that had turned green when Bernie activated it.

"I've never seen one of those before," mused Digit. "Must be something the New York agents developed."

The doctor placed it in his lab-coat pocket, which was exactly what Bernie hoped he would do.

"Enough delays; let's commence the test, shall we?" croaked the doctor.

"Do your worst," said Bernie confidently.

CHAPTER 20

S he didn't run. Panicking now would probably mean death.

Bernie wiped the sweat off her forehead as she crept carefully down the corridor, keeping her back to the wall and sliding along it as much as possible.

She'd read once that the secret to solving mazes is "wall-following," that if someone keeps contact with one wall the entire time, it should eventually lead to the exit. However, she also knew that it didn't apply if the "exit" was at the center.

But she didn't really have a choice except to try it.

One foot at a time, no sudden moves, she thought. The corridor she was following had wound twice to the right and once to the left. So far, she hadn't run into any of the challenges Dr. Thornpaw had hinted at.

Bernie glanced up to the balcony. She was relieved to

see that nobody was there. However, it didn't necessarily mean that the doctor wasn't watching from a remote location. So far, she hadn't spotted any cameras, but they could have been cleverly hidden.

She heard something—a low, mechanical hum from somewhere to her left. Bernie peeked around the corner.

SLASH!

A giant, razor-sharp scalpel sped downward like a guillotine. Bernie leaped back and found that if she had reacted one second slower, she would have been sliced neatly in half, becoming nothing more than a dissection experiment!

The scalpel receded back into a hidden compartment in the wall. Bernie realized that she'd been holding her breath and released it in a gasp. Her heart was flopping around in her chest like an electrocuted frog's.

Okay, good reminder. Don't let your guard down for a single minute! she thought.

She removed her hand from the wall just long enough to walk carefully around the area where the blade had sliced. She made a mental note about the whirring sound she'd heard just before the knife fell. Maybe it was a tiny bit of advance notice that would happen the next time something terrible was about to happen.

Next time, she'd be ready.

She returned her hand to the wall and hadn't taken

but a few steps more before she noticed something mounted to the wall in front of her. She crept carefully toward it and saw that it was a code written on a small brass plaque, something obviously designed to test her intellect.

It could be a trap, she thought. But in a way, it didn't matter. Even though Jarvis was the one picked for his code-cracking skills, Bernie loved puzzles. She would never allow herself to pass up an opportunity to do a puzzle and would always regret it if she didn't at least give it a try.

SGGA RGVF

Two words, Bernie thought. *Are the letters arranged out of order?* At first, she tried the substitution code, but that didn't work. Or was it a different language altogether?

She let her mind wander, allowing the letters to take on abstract shapes in her mind. She twisted them this way and that, freeing her subconscious mind to make associations. There was definitely something . . . something strange about them that was also kind of familiar. For some reason her thoughts turned to Jarvis. He was good at computers and was even better at codes than she was. Instead of feeling jealous like she had before, though, she found herself admiring him for that gift. She was sure he would have solved this code by now.

Then it hit her.

Occam's razor. The simplest solution is usually the best. That's what Jarvis had told her back at Mouse Watch HQ in LA. She thought of him typing the code on the computer, coming up with the most obvious password a mouse might think of.

And then, she had an inspiration.

She reached into her pocket and found a stub of a pencil. Thankfully, she'd pocketed it that morning when she thought she might have to take notes at orientation. Even though she would *never* forget the training she had gotten today, she had a good use for the pencil now.

She imagined a computer keyboard and wrote out the letters as her fingers mechanically did a basic typing of the QWERTY alphabet as written there.

QWERTYUIOPASDFGHJKLZXCVBNM

And then she added a regular, ordered alphabet underneath.

ABCDEFGHIJKLMNOPQRSTUVWXYZ

When she drew a line from each of the letters in the top row down to the ones on the bottom, she had something interesting.

Now, let's see if I'm right.

Bernie took the letters SGGA RGVF and translated them. Sure enough, a message was revealed:

LOOK DOWN.

She turned her gaze to the floor and noticed a very small button, hidden so carefully that if she hadn't been looking for it, she would have missed it.

Should she push it?

This was definitely where things got tricky. It could be a trap. Or, it could be her way out of there.

But she couldn't help herself. Bernie was a born button pusher.

She pushed her paw against it quickly, and then jumped back, just in case.

A thin, hairline crack appeared, forming the shape of a square. Then the square swung open downward, revealing a hidden staircase that led beneath the floor.

"Now, I wonder what horrible things are lurking for me down there?" she whispered anxiously.

She wished she had her new motorcycle. She imagined blasting through all the obstacles in front of her at a hundred miles per hour. It really would have come in handy right then.

Bernie took a deep, steadying breath and then tiptoed slowly down the stairs. At first, everything was pitch-dark. But then, after about ten steps, little LED lights flickered on near the staircase, illuminating the rest of her path down.

She tested each stair with her paw before going to the next one. But when she finally reached the bottom, a sound caused her to stop in her tracks.

This time, it wasn't the whir of machinery.

It was a voice. The voice of someone she knew!

Bernie peered around the corner and saw a row of cells.

Inside the one closest to her, packed like sardines, were all the members of the Los Angeles Mouse Watch!

Her heart leaped with relief when she saw the bright red hair of a particular agent that she'd been worried about.

"Alph!" squeaked Bernie.

The red-haired mouse glanced up, astonished. She rushed to the glass and pressed her paws against it. "Bernie! Is that really you?"

Bernie put her paws on the glass on the other side of Alph's.

"It's me. How long have you been in here?" she asked.

"We've been here for hours, ever since we were ambushed and captured from HQ," said Alph. "We were locked down here and haven't seen a single guard since then."

"We've got to get you out of here," said Bernie. "Is there a lock?"

"Over there," said Alph. "It's a numerical keypad. We've tried all kinds of combinations but none of us have been able to work it out."

"Hmm. Mind if I try?" asked Bernie.

"Be our guest," said Alph.

Bernie went over to the numerical switch-plate control and examined it closely. She wished she had Jarvis with her right then. He would have had the little machine he'd used before to crack the numerical lock of the Situation Room.

Bernie sighed.

The trouble with numerical codes is that there are thousands of possible combinations. But since she was fresh off her last puzzle, her mind was already working in overdrive. Maybe if she examined it closely, she'd find some secret to it.

At first, she didn't see anything out of the ordinary. But then, after studying it for a few minutes and punching a few numbers, she noticed that each number produced its own unique tone—kind of like a musical note.

Wait a second, she thought. *If the doctor created each obstacle in the maze with a possible solution, one designed to test the intelligence of the subject, then this is no accident. The notes are part of the code.*

Bernie played around with the different tones, trying to figure out what songs could be created by pressing the different notes. She hit the number four a couple of times. It reminded her of the song "Yankee Doodle."

After a bit of fiddling, she'd figured out the simple melody. But afterward, she was disappointed to see that nothing had happened.

"Nice tune," said Alph. "Can I ask why you're making songs instead of working out the combination?"

"I think it might be a musical lock," said Bernie. "If we could figure out the right song to make with the keys, maybe it would open the cell door."

"I would have never thought of that idea," admitted

Alph. "Let's all put our minds to it and see what we come up with."

Another agent, a bespectacled female wearing a red jumpsuit, suggested, "Since the range of notes is limited, there's only so many songs that might work. Maybe we should try simple ones."

As the agents began to brainstorm, Bernie felt no need to resist. Earlier, she would have insisted that she didn't need help, that she could do it herself. She would have been intent on making an identity for herself as a code breaker, competing with Jarvis. But after her humiliating encounter with the doctor, she'd learned her lesson.

"Okay, let's hear some ideas," Bernie said.

"I wonder if the song should correspond to something we need? Like, something with, I don't know, 'key' in the title?" asked Alph.

"Good idea," said Bernie excitedly. "That makes sense!"

But nobody could think of a single song with "key" in the title. After a few more minutes of trying, the happy mood grew somber.

"I just want to go home," said Stan, a thin, worried-looking mouse. "I'm tired of not being able to see a solution."

"Wait, what if that's it!" said Bernie, suddenly excited. "It would be just like Dr. Thornpaw to think that we mice couldn't *see* the solution right in front of our faces!"

"What is it?" asked Alph.

"Watch and see," said Bernie.

After a couple of missed notes, Bernie figured out what she wanted to play. It was a song she'd learned when she was very young. It was also a song that applied to all of their blind attempts at trying to solve the puzzle.

Bernie's fingers danced over the numbers, pressing them as if she were playing a piano or organ.

684, 684, 9554, 9554

"Three Blind Mice . . ." she sang.

There was a loud click.

The glass door slid open.

And the chamber echoed with cheers!

"We did it!" said Bernie.

"Let's get out of here," said Alph. Then she winked at Bernie and gave her a playful punch. "Good job, rookie!"

And Bernie felt happier than she had in ages. It was a brand-new feeling for her to work with a team and, she had to admit, it was also a whole lot more fun.

The group found a door at the end of the cells, and after going through it, found themselves entering a new part of the maze. This time, the walls weren't opaque white. Instead, the walls in this part were made of shiny glass and mirrors that distorted their reflections and those of the walls around them. Looking at them made her feel dizzy. But when she looked at the floor, she felt grounded again.

The best way to get out is to look at the floor! Bernie thought. *The glass and mirrors are a confusing illusion, but the floor is solid and can show us the way out.*

Bernie shared her revelation with the group. Working together, they managed to carefully make their way through the twisting maze, and for a moment it seemed like there wouldn't be any more obstacles. But then, just as Bernie thought that they might be getting close to an exit, they turned a corner and were met with a terrible sight.

The maze opened up into a gigantic room. A dozen whirring saw blades emerged from slots in the floor and ceiling, swinging in deadly arcs and spinning backward and forward like pendulums. Each one was armed with sharp, ruthless teeth.

The roar of the machinery was deafening.

"Those blades seem to be moving in a specifically coordinated pattern," said Alph. "Back and forth, see? Greg, can you design an algorithm that gives us the timing on them?"

"On it," said Greg. He was an older mouse with a very large, pink nose who spoke in a nasal tone. Seconds later, the math expert had scribbled a formula on a notepad and handed it back to Alph. Bernie took one look at the equation, noting the elegance of the solution, and thought about her father.

Clarence loved a well-constructed math problem.

"Okay, so if we follow this algorithm and time it just

right on our watches, we should each be able to run across. The key will be to coordinate our smart watches so that everyone moves precisely. One wrong step and . . . well, I don't need to say it," cautioned Alph.

"Um, excuse me," said Bernie, raising her paw.

"You don't have to raise your paw, Bern," said Alph.

"I don't have a smart watch," she confessed. "Remember, I'm not a Level One agent yet."

Alph looked surprised. "Wait, you're telling me that you didn't get my note?"

"What note?" asked Bernie.

"The one I left in your room for you and Jarvis," said Alph. "I know that technically it is against protocol, but when we were ambushed by R.A.T.S. I managed to send a message from my watch to the Candroid in your room. It was supposed to relay it to you guys." She looked concerned. "You're telling me you never got it? You must have been going out of your minds with worry!"

Bernie felt a surge of disappointment. If she hadn't been in such a big hurry to rush into action, she would have checked her room before leaving!

"I didn't go there," she said with a shrug. "But now I sure wish I had."

Everyone was quiet for a moment while they decided what to do. Without a watch, Bernie knew that it would be impossible to time her movements so that she could make it.

"You guys should go," said Bernie. She tried to sound as brave as she could, but her voice shook a little when she said it. "I'll stay here. It's more important to save the world than to worry about me."

The other agents stared at her for a long moment. Then, to Bernie's surprise, they all burst out laughing.

"What's so funny?" asked Bernie, puzzled.

Alph put an arm around her shoulders. "You still don't get it, do ya, rookie?" She turned to the group and said, "What do we say to that, gang?"

As one, the entire group recited, smiling, *"Every part of a watch is important, from the smallest gear on up. For without each part working together, keeping time is impossible. We never sleep. We never fail. We are there for all who call upon us in their time of need. We are the MOUSE WATCH!"*

Alph turned to Bernie and grinned. "We never, ever leave an agent behind, Skampersky. Don't you forget it."

Bernie was so happy she felt tears spring into her eyes. She hadn't wanted to admit how scary the prospect of being left behind had been. She couldn't find the words to say it, but she nodded gratefully.

Bernie looked at the formidable task ahead. Her instincts told her that this obstacle was probably the hardest part of the maze and that, if they succeeded in passing it, then the exit was on the other side.

At least she hoped she was right about that.

As a group, everyone was throwing out possible ideas of how to get Bernie across when suddenly, without warning, the blades slowed to a stop and powered down. Everyone gazed slack-jawed at the now receding death trap. Was this a part of the trick? Would they walk across, only to be sliced to smithereens by Dr. Thornpaw's tricky maze?

Then, as the largest of the spinning blades receded, Bernie saw a tall figure standing behind it. It was a rat! No, it was—

"Jarvis!" Bernie shouted.

The lanky rat grinned.

He shrugged and said, "That test looked pretty hard. Thought I might as well hack it."

Bernie ran across the floor and fell into his arms. While hugging him she said, "I'm happy to see you!" Then, she grinned widely. "Jarvis, you broke a rule! You came to save us!"

Jarvis blushed bright pink and said awkwardly, "I followed you. I couldn't let you get thrown out of the Watch all by yourself. What kind of a friend would I be if I let that happen?"

Bernie realized it was the first time he, or anyone else that she could remember, referred to her as a "friend." And it felt really, really good to have found one at last, in the most unlikely of places, with the most unlikely of animals.

CHAPTER 21

After a hasty reunion, the Watchers followed Jarvis to the wall of the maze that he'd blasted through. There was a big, jagged hole in it that was dripping with hot, melty, smelly cheese. Bernie couldn't help but smile.

"Stinky cheese bomb?"

Jarvis grinned back. "You know it. Turns out they have a *huge* stash of them here." Then he turned to the group. "Before I followed Bernie, I was able to contact the director. Right now, he and the major are somewhere here, looking for Dr. Thornpaw. If we hurry, we can finish the mission," Jarvis said.

"But how?" said Alph. "We're outnumbered and unarmed."

Reaching into his pocket, he produced a tiny vial that contained a bubbling blue chemical.

"What's that?" asked Bernie.

"The antidote to the cheese spray," said Jarvis. "While we were tracking down the sprayer, the director got ahold of Gadget. She synthesized the antidote and had it sent over. We've got to get it to the big tank of the doctor's formula—he's using it to fill the drones. If we succeed, he'll fill them with this."

"Brilliant!" said Bernie.

"Okay, let's stick together," said Alph. "Everyone be on the lookout for guards and if you see any weapons, grab them."

Bernie wished she could go and fight Dr. Thornpaw herself. She longed to have revenge! But she also didn't have to be reminded about the importance of relying on her team. "Where's the fueling tank?" she asked.

"I saw it on the way in," said Jarvis. "Follow me."

As they crept along the outside of the maze, Bernie noticed that if Jarvis hadn't cut a hole in the side, she would have never escaped.

There was no exit at all.

I should have known better, thought Bernie. There was no way a dangerous villain like Dr. Thornpaw would have ever let one of his experiments escape. Jarvis had, once again, solved the problem in the easiest way.

Occam's razor. Simplest solution. If there's a maze without an exit, blast a hole in the wall.

Bernie would remember that solution for a long time.

Soon they reached the platform upon which the doctor and Digit had been standing earlier. Bernie pulled Alph aside.

"What is it, Bern?" asked Alph.

"I don't know how to say this," whispered Bernie. "But Digit is working with Dr. Thornpaw. He was the spy."

Alph nodded thoughtfully. "You know what? It makes total sense."

"I thought you'd be angry!" said Bernie, surprised.

"Oh, I'm angry, that's for sure. But there was something about him lately, something I couldn't put my finger on." Her expression hardened. "After all this is over, we'll deal with him."

Alph reached into a hidden pocket in her uniform and removed a small silver weapon. She handed it to Bernie and said, "If you get into trouble, use this."

Bernie took it and stared at it curiously. "What does it do?"

"It fires a sonic pulse at your enemy. It's more powerful than it looks," Alph said.

"I thought I wasn't allowed to use any weapons," Bernie said.

"It's not a weapon," said Alph. "It's a really powerful gadget."

"But what about you?" asked Bernie. "You might need this."

Alph winked and said, "Don't worry about me, rookie. I just need you to watch your back out there. Remember to use your goggles and, if you get into trouble, use the A.I. interface to call for help." Bernie was grateful that Thornpaw hadn't taken her goggles away. Because they'd been in sleep mode, they looked ordinary. She guessed that he'd simply thought they were an innocent part of her uniform.

Bernie lowered them over her eyes and turned them back on.

"Wherever you are, the GPS in those babies will tell us how to track you down. We've got ya," said Alph. Bernie nodded, grateful for the advice and the weapon.

She followed Alph and the others as they rounded the corner of a walkway, which looked out over a vast chamber. Crouching low so that he wouldn't be seen, Jarvis indicated the enormous metal vat on the far side of the room. Bernie noticed something else and gasped. On a nearby platform just above them were a hundred gleaming white drones. *The Mouse Watch's stolen fleet!* The doctor's formula flowed through long tubes that were connected to each drone. When those drones flew over the city, it would turn every person in the city—or as far as the drones could fly—into a rat-obeying zombie.

Bernie noticed that a group of lab rats in white coats was patrolling the area.

"We need a diversion," said Alph. She turned to other agents. "Okay, here's what we'll do. Jarvis and Bernie will deliver the antidote to the tank while we distract the guards. Who's up for some fun?"

The other agents nodded without hesitation. Bernie couldn't help but admire their courage. From the smallest to the tallest, they were all truly the bravest mice ever born.

Alph spotted a large, human-size crowbar. It took several agents to lift it. After they hoisted it aloft, she called out to the guards in a voice that was loud and daring, "HEY! You guys looking for a fight?"

Five goggled heads turned in her direction. Together, the agents tossed the crowbar down below. The surprised rats barely managed to scamper away before it hit the tiles with a reverberating *CLANG!*

Alph leaped down the remaining stairs to the platform with a crowd of roaring agents behind her, all yelling "FOR THE WATCH!" at the top of their lungs.

Bernie watched as they bravely ran into danger. She tried to reassure herself by remembering that Alph and her team had probably done this hundreds of times.

"Come on, now's our chance!" hissed Jarvis. He indicated a nearby drone. Reaching into his pocket, he took out the Mouse Watch Drone Summoner that he'd gotten at the EEK. He pressed the button and the drone took off, racing toward the source of the signal. Seconds later, it made a perfect landing right next to them.

"Let's hop in that thing and get over to the vat," Bernie said. The two of them ran over to the vehicle as fast as they could. Jarvis had clambered inside and Bernie was about to go in, too, when a familiar voice called out: "Stop right there!"

Bernie turned.

It was Digit. The old Watcher wore a cruel expression and carried a dangerous-looking weapon in his paws. He aimed it at Bernie and said, "Well, well, well . . . a misfit mouse and a renegade rat. I have to say, I've taken down harder targets. Any last words?"

"Not for you!" said Bernie. "GO!" she yelled at Jarvis. Then, without a second thought for her own safety, she launched herself at Digit.

CHAPTER 22

Whether it was because he wasn't expecting it, or because he'd grown a little old and soft, Digit was caught off guard by Bernie's crazed attack.

Bernie, of course, didn't know any cool fighting moves. She didn't even know how to throw a single kick or a punch! But, just like she'd done with the terrier in Union Station, she knew that sometimes the best way to face a threat is to show no fear at all. She roared at the top of her lungs, and for a split second doubt flashed across Digit's eyes. He stumbled backward, tripping on one of the fuel lines connected to the nearest drone.

As he fell backward, Bernie saw something attached to his belt. It was the zip-line grappling hook he'd been carrying on her very first day. She couldn't believe it had only been the day before!

Without a second thought she grabbed it, and then, thinking fast, she shot the zip line up to the drone that Jarvis was flying. It caught on the drone's landing gear and immediately whisked Bernie up into the air. But just as she was being pulled upward, she felt an iron grip on her ankle, yanking her back.

Looking down, Bernie saw Digit hanging below her with a ferocious grin on his face. The weight of the bulky mouse made her leg feel like it was being pulled out of its socket. She kicked and struggled but nothing she could do would shake him loose.

As Jarvis tried to pilot the wobbling drone toward the vat, Bernie felt herself swinging wildly. The sky around her spun dizzily, and the ground seemed to be miles below, plus the pain in her leg was growing unbearable! Even though they were high up in the air, Digit just wouldn't let go!

She gulped and held on for dear life as the speeding vehicle zoomed around the huge laboratory. She caught a glimpse of the floor below, noting that Alph and the Mouse Watch agents were battling hard with the R.A.T.S. Beakers of colorful, glowing chemicals crashed to the floor.

Suddenly, the vat swung into view, bubbling with the doctor's orange formula. Bernie was losing her grip with the added weight, and she feared that she was going to fall at any moment. As Jarvis tried to steady the pitching drone, Bernie heard him call down, "Bernie! I feel bad about something!"

"Jarvis, it's okay to break the rules this one time," she shouted back.

"No, I mean, I should have gone with you back at the ferry. I . . . I chickened out and I wanted to say I'm sorry! I still tried to help you, though."

"Don't be sorry! I'm the one who's sorry! I never should have doubted you!" Bernie called to him. Her hands were slipping now. She knew that if she died, at least she would have mended everything. "You're one of us, Jarvis. I hope you know that I know that now. And . . . more importantly, you're my friend!"

Jarvis beamed down at her as he removed something from his pocket. It was a small bottle with a red cap. Inside of it was a liquid that Bernie couldn't identify. "Hey, Bernie?" said Jarvis.

"What?" said Bernie.

"Do you trust me?"

"I'm swinging from a plane you're flying!" said Bernie. "I think the answer is yes!" Her arms were really hurting now and her leg was hurting even more. Digit was laughing maniacally as he began to pull himself upward, using Bernie's leg like a rope.

Jarvis unscrewed the cap of the little bottle. "If you trust me, then DUCK!"

Jarvis took careful aim and shook the bottle. Bernie did as she was told, and as she turned her head away, she saw a drop of something from the bottle shoot past her. It wasn't one of Thornpaw's chemicals.

It wasn't even something from the EEK.

Whatever it was, the bright red juice flew right into Digit's open, laughing mouth. His eyes grew wide. He sputtered and coughed. He reacted like he'd been stung, and with a yelp of pain, he released Bernie's leg and fell down, down, down into the bubbling vat of orange liquid below.

"Ahhh!" he cried, and then, "Mmm, it *tastes* like cheese, too!" Digit sputtered and flailed as he tried to slurp up the doctor's secret formula.

"What was that?" shouted Bernie.

"TABASCO SAUCE!" Jarvis yelled happily.

Bernie could hardly believe it! Without the added weight pulling her down, she scampered up the zip line to the cockpit. After Jarvis pulled her in, he said, "I hope they won't mind that I borrowed it from the kitchen at HQ."

She gave him a hug.

It turned out, rats gave great hugs.

"I'm sure they won't! Now hurry! Drop the antidote!"

Jarvis quickly dumped the vial of blue liquid into the insidious brew.

"There it goes!" he said. The vial turned the entire mixture from orange to purple, and as the mist from Gadget's spray filled the air, Digit's eyes closed. The wicked mouse stopped struggling as Gadget's Sleep Spray slowly took its effect, and he released a loud snore.

"We did it!" shouted Bernie.

"Well, what do we do now?" Jarvis asked.

"Well, I'm hoping New York HQ got the homing signal from my hair clip and that agents are on their way here to help us get Thornpaw and clean up this mess. But just in case . . ."

Jarvis shot her a worried glance.

"Listen, Jarvis, he killed my brother. I need to confront Thornpaw face-to-face. I promise I'm not being impulsive, I'm just doing what's right. I need to do this, Jarvis. Please?"

Jarvis held the control stick of the drone for a second and stared straight ahead out the cockpit window. Then he turned to Bernie and said in a firm, supportive voice, "I'm in," and added, "But where is he? I didn't see him anywhere in the lab."

"I know where we'll find him. Where's the Bluetooth system on this thing?"

Jarvis indicated the touch screen next to the navigation system. Bernie did a quick search for any transmitting signals and squealed in delight when HAIRCLIP77 popped up for pairing. She selected it, and moments later a blue dot showed exactly where the homing beacon was located.

"He's there!" shouted Bernie.

Jarvis did a sharp turn and sent the drone speeding in the direction of the flashing dot. They flew along the long laboratory corridor and down a sprawl of equipment-laden storage rooms, coming eventually to a richly appointed, human-size office. Thankfully, the door was open a tiny crack, but it was just big enough for the drone to fit through. Inside they saw the rat they were looking for.

Thornpaw watched the approach of the buzzing drone with a surprised look on his face. Jarvis swept down within a foot or so of where he stood, and he grabbed the handset for the P.A. system.

"Give it up, Thornpaw. We have you," Jarvis said.

Now that they were close, Thornpaw could see who was piloting the vehicle. His scarred face split into a wide, yellow-toothed grin. Bernie then noticed with a horrible sinking feeling that several of the New York agents were tied up in chairs, waiting to inhale whatever foul, mind-altering chemical it was that the doctor had concocted.

Bernie gasped when she saw the major, one of the toughest agents she'd met so far, tied up and first in line. The doctor had overpowered her, and he didn't seem to have endured the slightest scratch! The major, on the other hand, had two black eyes and one of her wrists hung limply by her side.

Seeing a hero who spent her life fighting to protect others tied up filled Bernie with rage.

"You're going to pay for this!" shouted Bernie.

Thornpaw's grin spread even wider when he saw the look of hatred wash over Bernie's face. He removed a cloth from his pocket and casually wiped down the razor-sharp blades of his claw. "I'll enjoy this," he said.

A feeling of pure rage consumed Bernie. She didn't really realize what she was doing. She heard Jarvis somewhere in the background, shouting as she leaped from the drone and flew down the three-foot drop toward the evil doctor, landing perfectly on all four paws. All she could think about at that moment was Brody. She could see his kind and gentle face more clearly than ever in her mind as she switched on her goggles and grabbed the sonic blaster that Alph had given her.

"This is for Brody!" she shouted.

She was oblivious to her own danger as she fell directly on top of the doctor, knocking him to the ground. She pounded him with her little fists and kicked him with her feet. She bit and scratched. She was far more animal than intelligent mouse right then, but all she could see was red.

She took the blaster in paw and was about to fire it when Thornpaw's giant metal claw knocked it out of her paw with a quick, well-aimed strike. Her heart sank as she heard the sonic weapon clatter away in the distance.

The doctor laughed.

Bernie realized that Thornpaw wasn't hurt at all

from her wild attack. The villain vaulted skyward, using his hydraulic legs to his advantage. "You little fool." He laughed. "You really think that you could take on an evolutionary marvel like myself?"

Bernie was breathing hard. She was frustrated. She was angry. Her tail was stiff as a knitting needle.

And, unfortunately for her, Thornpaw's mechanical enhancements gave him a significant advantage when fighting any ordinary mouse. The doctor leaped at her and slashed out with his claw.

Bernie's goggles alerted her in the nick of time. The warning was just enough for her to duck the swipe, but she wasn't fast enough to avoid it entirely. She felt a searing pain in her shoulder as she tumbled to the ground. It wasn't enough to completely disable her, but it hurt terribly.

The doctor executed a perfect landing and paused, a gloating expression on his face as he saw Bernie gripping her wounded shoulder.

"I've fought enemies much larger than you, Bernie Skampersky. In fact"—he chuckled—"they were ALL larger than you. In what world do you think a tiny, helpless mouse like yourself could defeat me? I am more than a rat. I am the future!"

The doctor loomed over Bernie and raised his cruel claw, about to strike.

This is it, thought Bernie. *This is where I die just like Brody.*

She closed her eyes tight, anticipating the killing blow.

But then, a loud, ear-shattering CLANG! stopped the doctor's claw in midair.

To Thornpaw and Bernie's surprise, a zip-line cable had appeared from nowhere and wrapped itself around the doctor in one well-aimed shot.

"What?" squawked the doctor.

Bernie saw Jarvis holding the other end of Digit's invention, with a look of sheer determination on his face. He'd left the drone on autopilot, leaping down from it to stand right beside her.

"Nobody talks to my friend that way!" shouted Jarvis. "She may be small, but she's MIGHTY!"

"Good job, Jarvis!" shouted Bernie, shaking with relief. And then, Bernie did something that she'd never done before. It was something that at one time she would have considered unthinkable.

She placed her finger on the side of her goggles and said to the A.I. interface, "Help! We've got Thornpaw. We need backup!"

"Idiots!" shouted Thornpaw. "You think that this stupid cable can hold me?" Bernie's eyes widened with alarm as she saw a metal saw emerge from the back of his claw and begin to spin, lowering toward the metal cable that had him trapped.

"Don't even try it!" came a chorus of new voices.

Thornpaw glanced down and saw a dozen laser sights dancing on his chest. Behind Bernie and Jarvis was a team of Mouse Watch agents, their blue goggles glowing and grim expressions on their brave faces.

Thornpaw's arrogant expression faded. It was clear that, for the first time, the evil doctor was facing certain defeat. The blade stopped spinning and returned to a hidden compartment in his metal claw.

Bernie, battered and bruised, clutched her wounded shoulder and shared a smile with Jarvis.

They had done it.

And, more importantly, they'd accomplished the impossible by working together. Never again would Bernie question Jarvis's loyalty. As she looked up at him, she saw something in his face and expression, something that reminded her of someone she'd known very, very well.

As Jarvis gazed down at her with his warm brown eyes, she didn't see a rat anymore. She saw someone who looked, surprisingly, an awful lot like Brody.

"You can call me *small but mighty* anytime you want to," said Bernie shyly.

Jarvis grinned and said, "Thanks. And you can call me anything you want to, except for one thing."

"Oh?" asked Bernie. "What's that?"

"Late for dinner," said Jarvis, grinning even more broadly. "I don't know about you, but I'm starving!"

CHAPTER 23

ernie had, of course, heard the saying that New York is "the city that never sleeps." That's why it was such a strange sight to see the entire city actually snoring. The population was sprawled out in a dreamless sleep, and, upon waking, would remember none of this nightmare, all thanks to Gadget Hackwrench.

While the human citizens slept, Bernie, Jarvis, and the rest of the Mouse Watch agents helped restore all that had been damaged under Dr. Thornpaw's brief but terrible reign.

Bernie and Jarvis worked as a team the whole time. Gadget herself emerged from her secret workshop to oversee the entire operation, carefully making sure that everything was put back exactly how it was, right down to the last lightbulb. Bernie's jaw dropped to the ground when Chip and Dale showed up to help, too!

The mood was jubilant. Everyone felt relieved that the mission had been accomplished and that the sleeping citizens' nightmares were finally over. When the people of New York City awoke, they would never know that somewhere, locked away in a very special fortified prison dedicated to the most nefarious of R.A.T.S. criminals, Dr. Thornpaw resided. He even had a new name. The nefarious villain was no longer a doctor of any kind, but instead simply known as inmate number 206.

The number was stitched onto the pocket of his prison jumpsuit.

It was a fate better than he deserved in many agents' opinions, but Gadget had made sure that the prison was outfitted with the latest in security technology and assured the agents that no one, not even an evil genius, could break free. And Thornpaw was hardly that.

The rest of Thornpaw's lab rats had given up quickly after their leader had been apprehended and were now in a minimum-security jail. The Mouse Watch believed in rehabilitation when possible, and they held out hope that the rats would mend their evil ways.

They all felt that if one rat could change sides and join the Mouse Watch, maybe others could, too.

When New York City was back to normal, the S.W.I.S.S. was waiting to take everyone back to California. Jarvis wasn't thrilled at the idea, but when he was offered a special motion-sickness capsule designed by Gadget for people of a more "delicate" constitution, he happily accepted it.

Bernie was relieved to be going back home. She missed her parents and wanted to tell them all about the amazing things that had happened. While they waited at the platform for the S.W.I.S.S. to arrive, she asked Jarvis a question she'd been wondering about.

"Hey, Jarvis?"

"Hmm?"

"You've never told me anything about your family," said Bernie.

Jarvis got a faraway look in his eyes. He sighed and shrugged his shoulders. "There's really not that much to tell. I had seven brothers and sisters and they all joined the R.A.T.S. We were poor and nearly starving. They do a lot of recruiting in our neighborhood, promising a better life, food, and shelter. When you've been a rat digging around in the garbage most of your life, it can sound pretty good at face value. I didn't believe it, of course, but my brothers and sisters did. I wouldn't have ever joined except . . ."

"Except for what?" Bernie asked gently.

Jarvis looked at Bernie and she noticed how much pain was in his eyes. "They took our parents and held them in prison cells. They told us that they would be killed if we didn't do exactly what they asked of us."

"That's terrible," said Bernie.

Jarvis nodded. "Yeah. They said that if I didn't use my computer skills to help them, my parents would suffer, so I did as I was told—that is, until I found out the truth."

Bernie was afraid to ask. Jarvis continued in a low, quiet voice, "My parents were already dead. They'd refused to join the R.A.T.S. and they were never put in prison at all. It was a lie. The R.A.T.S. did everything they could do to keep us afraid and working for them. Once I found out the truth, I left."

Bernie reached up high to put her hand on Jarvis's shoulder. He sniffled a little. Bernie swore to herself that she wouldn't stop with just Thornpaw. Any group that would do such a terrible thing to her best friend would be her enemy for life.

"You know what, Jar?" said Bernie.

"What?" said Jarvis.

"I'll never stop being your friend."

And Bernie could tell from the tears in his eyes that it was the nicest thing anyone had ever said to him.

CHAPTER 24

I t wasn't but a few days later that Bernie and Jarvis
sat together in the huge room where they'd been welcomed as new recruits. Everyone was in attendance,
and there was electricity in the air.

A very special announcement was about to be made.

"Can you believe this is real?" asked Bernie, punching
Jarvis playfully in the ribs.

"Ow! Yes. Painfully real, thanks!" Jarvis said.

They both laughed.

"Think about it!" Just a few days ago we were brand-new
recruits. And now—"

"We're still brand-new recruits," finished Jarvis.
"However, we have seen more action than a lot of the
experienced agents!" he said, his eyes twinkling.

"Oh, that's for sure," agreed Bernie. "Oh yeah, I forgot,
I smuggled something for you from the cafeteria."

Bernie reached under her chair and removed a small, covered container. Jarvis took it and opened the lid. His eyes grew wide as he thrust his nose inside, taking a long, exaggerated whiff.

"Cheese soufflé with Tabasco sauce!" he enthused. "How did you . . . ?"

"I made friends with the cook! She said she learned the recipe from an old cowboy mouse named Tabasco Johnson. Apparently, he loves Tabasco sauce as much as you do!"

Jarvis grinned. "Forget the ceremony! Let's get this over with so I can start eating!"

Bernie chuckled.

Every agent in the Watch could feel the excitement as the lights dimmed. This time, there was no hologram of Gadget. This time, Bernie's heroine was there in person, and as she took the stage grinning happily, everyone cheered along with Bernie, who was yelling the loudest.

"Welcome, everyone!" said Gadget. Bernie noticed that she was wearing her trademark periwinkle jumpsuit and goggles. Her work clothes were always on, and even on the most formal of occasions it seemed that she could never stop thinking of inventing something new and had to be constantly ready to grab a welder's torch or some electrical wire at a moment's notice.

"Well, as you know, it's a very special night," said Gadget. "Tonight, we're about to do something never before done in Mouse Watch history. Tonight, we're promoting two recruits to Level One agents before they've even gone through training."

Everyone cheered. Bernie had so much joy inside of her, she felt like she would pop.

"Would Bernie Skampersky and Jarvis Slinktail please come forward?"

Gadget motioned for Jarvis and Bernie to take the stage. As Bernie approached, she noticed that a couple of platforms rose from hidden recesses, displaying two official black-and-silver jumpsuits that were identical in every way, except that one was quite a bit taller and outfitted with a hood. Jarvis really liked hoods.

Bernie recalled that each jumpsuit had a color representing a different division of the Watch. Black with silver trim for special ops, gold for research and development, and crimson for interior security.

Black and silver had been what she was hoping for.

Special operations.

The coolest of the bunch!

She could hardly believe that it was finally happening.

As Bernie walked onto the stage and held the uniform that had been offered to her, she glanced down at her brand-new agent's watch, the one that Alph had instructed the Candroid to leave in her room, and noted the date and time next to the animated Mouse Watch agent.

6:48 p.m.

It was the moment she'd been waiting for her entire life.

"Congratulations, Bernie Skampersky and Jarvis Slinktail. Welcome to the Watch!" said Gadget.

The cheers that erupted from the crowd could have brought down the ceiling. Bernie blushed from the tip of her nose to the tip of her tail. She glanced out into the crowd and saw her parents, who had been invited for the special day and were beaming with pride.

Bernie's eyes blurred with happy tears. She knew that there was much to learn going forward, but with the help of the Watch to whom she'd sworn loyalty, she knew she could face whatever was to come.

She was finally part of a team.

Gadget ordered the houselights up and for everyone to stand. Then, Bernie Skampersky, along with the rest of the Mouse Watch, recited the oath she now believed in with all her heart.

It was more than just an oath.

It was a promise to herself and to everyone she would protect.

Every part of a watch is important, from the smallest gear on up. For without each part working together, keeping time is impossible. We never sleep. We never fail. We are there for all who call upon us in their time of need.

We are the MOUSE WATCH!

EPILOGUE

The paw looked like any other.

It wasn't scarred or misshapen.

It didn't have long, bony fingers with black nails.

The paw was, in fact, carefully manicured. And the rest of the body that it belonged to was the same . . . fastidious and clean. The creature's fur shone with health. The clothes it wore were sensible and designed to blend in wherever they were worn.

In fact, Kryptos didn't look like a creature who didn't possess a soul. The truth was, Kryptos didn't look like anything anyone would remember. The rodent appeared to be completely ordinary in every way.

Which was exactly how Kryptos wanted it.

"Your Eminence." A rat in a blue button-down shirt

and plain khaki pants stood in the doorway. "Word has come that Dr. Thornpaw has been incarcerated."

Kryptos released an almost imperceptible sigh. Thornpaw was of little consequence.

"The doctor was but a pawn on the chessboard. An idiot. I let him have his little mind-control experiment, and he failed, as I knew he would. He is too concerned with theatrics. Replacing humans with rats, ha! As if we want their paltry little lives. A house, a job—they are just cages. Bigger, yes, but cages all the same. Rats are meant for more. We deserve more."

Kryptos wandered over to a chess set on a table by his desk and moved a chess piece, knocking another one off the table. It rolled under the sofa. "I have other pieces to play, ones far more powerful."

He sat down at his desk and examined a file, scanning it carefully for any errors. Being meticulous was everything. Without careful scrutiny there were mistakes, and with mistakes, there was chaos. Kryptos didn't like chaos. He liked to be in control.

Mistakes were simply not allowed.

"Now," he said, looking up at his assistant. "Do you want to know what happens next?"

ACKNOWLEDGMENTS

I'd like to thank my editor, Jocelyn Davies, and her brilliant team at Disney Hyperion.

Jocelyn, your incredible imagination and skill made chronicling these mouse adventures a joy to write. You're truly the best. Thank you!

Also, as always, to my wife, Nancy, for her constant love and support. There's no world I could create that can match the incredible one I spend with you every day.

For the WATCH!

—J. J. Gilbert

Turn the page for a sneak peek at the
Mouse Watch's next adventure!

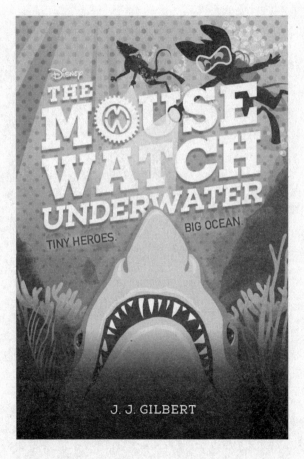

CHAPTER 1

Bernie Skampersky raced down the gleaming white corridor that led to the Secret Watcher International Subway System. She checked her watch. The display showed a cartoon version of herself running next to a countdown clock. The clock was synched with the S.W.I.S.S. station terminal.

Two minutes to the next train! she thought. *I'd better hustle!*

She doubled her speed, calling back to her fellow agent Jarvis Slinktail to try to keep up. Jarvis, in spite of being much taller than she was, preferred sitting behind a keyboard rather than doing anything physical whatsoever. The lanky rat was her best friend, and she noticed that his shock of blond hair bounced comically in his eyes as he huffed and puffed, trying to keep pace with her.

"Last one there is a R.A.T.S. agent!" Bernie shouted.

"Not . . . (huff) . . . fair!" Jarvis called back. "I had a . . . (puff) . . . huge breakfast! Cheddar-cheese waffles!"

Bernie chuckled. Jarvis's appetite was becoming legendary at Mouse Watch HQ. It had gotten so bad that the cafeteria mice had been known to panic and lock the cafeteria doors when they saw him coming.

Bernie was a short brown mouse with a haystack of blue hair and long eyelashes. Joining the Mouse Watch had been her dream, one that had actually come true when she'd been accepted to the elite band of agents six months ago.

As she ran, she noticed how much steadier her breathing had become and that her legs were much stronger than when she'd first joined up. With the rigorous training exercises she did every day, she was starting to gain athletic abilities she'd never known, and clad in her official Level One agent uniform, a black jumpsuit with silver trim, she looked every bit a part of the illustrious team.

Bernie ran toward the secret area indicated on the map on her goggles' screen. The smart goggles were one of the Watchers' most important instruments, a hi-tech piece of enhanced-reality gear that allowed an agent to do countless useful things, including, as Bernie was using it for right then, consulting a highly accurate mapping system. She'd only used the S.W.I.S.S. station once before, and because Mouse Watch HQ was such a vast, sprawling warren of glass windows and mazelike corridors, the map was quite helpful.

She scurried past the locker room that led to the gym and reached the drinking fountains well before Jarvis did. By the time he caught up, she remembered to use the switch behind the fountains to open the secret door.

"What took you so long?" asked Bernie.

Jarvis was huffing and puffing so hard that he couldn't answer for a full thirty seconds. "T- . . . too . . ."

"Too? Too what?" asked Bernie. "Too far to run?"

"Too . . . basco sauce," wheezed Jarvis. "I forgot to grab some on the way out. Just give me a second to run back. . . ."

"No time!" Bernie cried. "We're on a schedule! Somebody needs rescuing and we have to go!"

Jarvis shrugged and held out his paws in a helpless gesture. "What if I need a snack? Nothing tastes good without Tabasco anymore!" he exclaimed. "I even put it on my cereal this morning!"

"You have a problem," said Bernie. "Come on, someone's in serious danger!"

The secret door behind the drinking fountains led to a very old stairway in a crumbling, brick-lined tunnel. Bernie found it interesting because it was very unlike the rest of the conspicuously clean, futuristic Mouse Watch headquarters. She had no idea what the old tunnel had been used for originally. But, seeing how ancient and crumbly the bricks were, Bernie wondered if it was part of a much older building that had once stood where HQ now was. Apparently, sometime in the distant past of Los Angeles, someone had needed a stairway to access the old tunnels beneath the city.

It was very mysterious.

But Bernie liked to imagine that a secret society used to meet there, making plans to take over the world, or that it was possibly a hideout for robbers while they plotted some kind of bank heist.

It was impossible for her not to feel daring and adventurous when descending the rickety stairs.

When she reached the bottom, Bernie checked her watch and was happy to see that they'd actually arrived with two seconds to spare. Despite the Tabasco-related slowdown, their training was paying off.

Grinning, she showed Jarvis her record time. The lanky rat nodded but looked wholly unimpressed. "Good for you," he said, sounding tired.

"If you put as much effort into physical training as you do into eating, next time we can make even better time," said Bernie.

"No thank you," said Jarvis. "Running through obstacle courses—"

"Is a fun challenge?" finished Bernie, grinning.

"No," said Jarvis. "I was gonna say, 'is my least favorite thing in the world to do.' Besides," he added, glancing at her through his blond mop of hair, "I say anybody who wastes their time running around when they could be thinking or playing video games has a misplaced set of priorities."

Jarvis was brilliant with computers. Bernie was good at solving puzzles, but there had never been, in Mouse Watch history, anybody better at it than Jarvis. He was the most natural code breaker the Watch had ever seen. They'd made an exception for him to join up with them, in spite of the fact that he was a rat and had once (even though he hadn't wanted to) worked for R.A.T.S.—the Rogue Animal Thieves Society.

The group had a dark reputation. They knew how to take advantage of every angle, how to manipulate and exploit anybody who was weak and vulnerable. Jarvis had needed help and they'd offered to take care of him . . . for a price. R.A.T.S. was the most corrupt gang of evildoers ever assembled, and they worked tirelessly for their own selfish purposes.

That included destroying anybody who stood in their way.

R.A.T.S.—which was made up of more than just rats, including assorted other villainous vermin and sneaky reptiles—was the archnemesis of the Mouse Watch. The evil, covert group sought to destroy the Mouse Watch and take the world back from humans. Bernie shuddered, thinking of the last time she'd gone up against R.A.T.S., when they had taken over New York City and tried to drive all humans underground. If not for the intrepid Mouse Watch, Bernie felt sure that there wouldn't have been anyone left to stop their diabolical deeds.

Bernie's goggles lit up with a blue glow that cast an eerie light in the dim shadows. A series of pop-up balloons appeared in the corner of the screen with instructions for how to use the transport system.

> STEP ONE: SUMMON TRAIN USING VOICE COMMAND "HEY, S.W.I.S.S."
>
> STEP TWO: STATE DESTINATION.
>
> STEP THREE: AFTER BOARDING THE TRAIN, SELECT SPECIFIC DESTINATION FROM THE MENU.
>
> STEP FOUR: BUCKLE UP!

Loudly and clearly, Bernie said, "Hey, S.W.I.S.S.!"

An electronic female voice with a light British accent replied, "Coming!"

A few seconds later, the shiny white Maglev train slid soundlessly up to the station platform. As she watched it approach, Bernie thought about her last adventure. At that time, she'd had a strong prejudice against rats. When she was just a mouseling, she'd had a run-in with one named Dr. Thornpaw, a horrible villain who had outfitted himself with powerful robotic limbs to replace the ones human scientists had ruined through tests and experiments. The soulless Dr. Thornpaw had taken her brother Brody's life, and it had haunted Bernie ever since. But that wasn't the last time she saw Dr. Thornpaw—she encountered him again on her first day as a Mouse Watch agent. The evil doctor had vowed revenge on all of humanity, and he also turned out to be one of the most formidable opponents the Mouse Watch had ever faced. The mind-controlling cheese spray he'd developed had nearly taken down New York City, turning all the citizens into zombies. Thanks to Bernie and Jarvis, he'd been stopped in his tracks and was now safely behind bars.

Not bad for a couple of rookies! thought Bernie, smiling.

It really was an understatement. She hadn't trusted Jarvis at first, but all of Bernie's preconceived notions about rats had disappeared when he saved her and a team of Mouse Watch agents from a deadly maze in Dr. Thornpaw's lab. Ever since, they'd been best friends.

The doors whooshed open, and Bernie and Jarvis boarded the S.W.I.S.S. She couldn't help but notice that Jarvis looked particularly uneasy. His whiskers drooped and his furry complexion was pale. The first time he'd ridden the supersonic train he'd gotten violently sick. She felt a wave of concern.

"Hey, did you bring some of those . . ." Bernie began.

"Motion-sickness tablets that Gadget designed?" finished Jarvis. "Yeah. Right here."

Jarvis pulled one of the tablets out of his pocket and popped it in his mouth. "At least it tastes like Tabasco-covered cheese," he said, chewing. "That's about the only good thing I can think of when riding this stupid train."

He raised the hood on his uniform and retreated within it like a turtle going into its shell. Jarvis's uniform matched Bernie's except for that necessary addition. Jarvis loved hoods, and the Watch had kindly customized his jumpsuit to accommodate his favorite accessory.

The two Watchers found their seats, stowed their backpacks beneath them, and secured their safety harnesses. The electronic female voice said, "Please state your destination."

"Portland, Oregon," said Bernie.

"Portland station," replied the S.W.I.S.S. "Please be sure your restraints are properly fastened. Arrival time, T minus three minutes, twenty-six seconds."

Bernie and Jarvis had barely fastened the buckles on their harnesses when, with a sonic *BOOM!* the train shot down the tracks like a bullet from a gun.

As the mouse-size train flew down the rails, navigating old sewer tunnels that intersected with the Watch's specially constructed new ones, Bernie thought of how different her current reality was compared to her old one.

Back in Thousand Acorns, her hometown, mice had to make the most out of everyday objects. For example, a thimble might make a good bowl for soup. A bottle cap could be an end table. And just about anything that could be salvaged from a toy store or a fashion doll's wardrobe could be reimagined or altered to fit a mouse. It was creative but always just a little bit uncomfortable.

Now that she was an agent at the Mouse Watch, she enjoyed all kinds of new, mouse-size comforts and devices. This was definitely thanks to Gadget Hackwrench, the head inventor and leader of the organization. Gadget was a legend from her days working with Chip and Dale's Rescue Rangers, and Bernie had studied everything there was to know about her hero, including her early inventions, like the Ranger Plane.

Since breaking off from the Rescue Rangers and starting her own organization, Gadget had progressed with the times and had turned her genius brain to developing the amazing tiny tech and miniature comforts that the Mouse Watch now relied upon. Bernie never knew how great life could be until she'd become a Watcher. She was living the dream, even though her new life was also filled with danger.

But for her, danger added a little spice.

Not so much for Jarvis. The only spice he craved could be found in a small bottle of hot sauce.

That, and solving a good puzzle.

As if on cue, Bernie's watch pinged, alerting her that the timetable for her rescue operation was ticking away. When on a mission, the smart watch counted down rather than up, and she noticed that she only had thirty minutes to complete the task.

She felt nervous. Bernie had no idea who they were going to rescue, but she knew that it must have been a really important mission to have such a short and urgent countdown to get there. A thirty-minute rescue meant that it was a top priority. Someone was most certainly in immediate danger.

Well, they assigned the right rodents to the job, Bernie thought. She and Jarvis were both eager to prove themselves.

Even though the S.W.I.S.S. was incredibly fast, Bernie couldn't help but wish it could go even faster. Every agent would be evaluated on their mission performance and, although she'd never been a stellar student in school back home, here at the Mouse Watch she was determined to get top marks as a Level One recruit.

Almost as quickly as it had begun, the train ride was ending. Bernie reached for the straps of her backpack as the train slowed, anxious to bolt out of the doors and get to the address on her smart watch display.

"Mount Tabor Park," she murmured. The watch showed that the Portland neighborhood was about twenty minutes from the Portland Mouse Watch terminal. In order to get there on time they were going to have to really move.

"Better get your Pop! Cycle ready, Jarvie," said Bernie. "We've got a race ahead of us. . . ."

"Do you really have to call me that?" mumbled Jarvis. "It sounds so babyish."

Bernie glanced over to Jarvis, who was slouching in his seat, arms folded across his chest and his hoodie pulled low over his eyes.

"Jar?"

"Mmmgh," said Jarvis.

Bernie pulled back his hood so she could see his face. The skinny rat stared at her with his big brown eyes. Bernie could tell that, in spite of the motion sickness pills, he looked a little queasy.

"You okay?" asked Bernie.

"Ugh," said Jarvis, sitting up. "I hate these stupid trains. Why couldn't Gadget invent some kind of dematerializing transport device, one that would go *BRZZZT!* and your atomic particles would be immediately reassembled wherever you wanted to go?"

"I'm no scientist, but turning yourself into a bunch of random particles sounds like a bad idea," said Bernie.

"Although, if anybody could figure out how to do it, Gadget could. Hey, I've got some water in my backpack. You can drink it if you think it will help settle your stomach."

Jarvis shook his head and motioned her away. "Thanks, but I'll be okay. Just get me back on solid ground."

Bernie felt the train glide to a stop as it approached the Portland terminal, and a few seconds later the door slid open and the voice said, "Arrived. Please disembark."

Without hesitation, Jarvis grabbed his backpack and they both rushed out the door. Unlike New York's Grand Central Terminal platform, the Portland stop was a very simple affair, just a brick platform beneath a manhole cover. Bernie spotted a mouse-size iron ladder that had been installed next to a small doorway.

She checked her watch. "We've only got eighteen minutes! Hurry!"

"Seriously, Bern," groused Jarvis. "How does the S.W.I.S.S. not affect you at ALL?"

"I have a very sturdy constitution. I think it may be part of why I got recruited."

It was true. Bernie was small, but she was mighty. Nothing kept her down for long. Even a broken leg hadn't stopped her from traveling all the way to the Mouse Watch headquarters for her first day on the job.

Bernie led the way, scrambling up the tiny ladder and emerging through the door into an old back alley. Outside, the fall weather felt cool and crisp. The sky was dotted with a few dark clouds, but between them, the late-afternoon sun shone through. According to the map in her goggles' display, they'd emerged at a spot near the Hawthorne Bridge, a spectacular truss bridge that spanned the massive Willamette River.

The sun's fading rays sparkled on the water, dazzling their eyes. If they'd had the time, Bernie would have loved to scamper along the banks of the river with Jarvis and maybe find a spot for a picnic—hidden away from human eyes, of course. In that brief daydream, Bernie would have brought plenty of Tabasco sauce, and she and Jarvis would have spent a lovely afternoon joking and laughing as the sun went down.

It was a beautiful thought. But there was no time for goofing around. Someone important was in serious danger.

"Let's ride," said Bernie, lowering her goggles. "We're—"

"Burning daylight. I know," finished Jarvis.

With a practiced motion, they reached into their nylon backpacks and retrieved aluminum cylinders, which snapped apart with a *POP!* A gleaming, futuristic-looking pod shot out from each tube, unfolding automatically into a mouse-size motorcycle.

Bernie never got tired of Gadget's tech. It was like magic. Her boss really was amazing.

VROOOAOOWWW! Bernie hit the gas hard with her hind paw, and the engine revved into gear. The map to Mount Tabor appeared on her goggles as she rocketed down the scenic Portland city streets, sticking to shadows cast by the curbs. Jarvis followed close behind.

Bernie watched the countdown clock in the corner of her screen and winced. This one was gonna be close!

She increased her speed. Bernie knew that anyone who might have been looking in their direction would have seen two very tiny figures weaving in and out of gutters and next to sidewalk curbs, avoiding random pieces of litter and the occasional pothole or crack. They would have perhaps mistaken the two small riders for a couple of normal, if fast-moving, rodents, or exceptionally large low-flying insects. Bernie knew that only the most observant among the humans would have been amazed to see that they were really a mouse and a rat, each clothed in tiny jumpsuits, rocketing down the street on custom high-tech motorcycles.

Gadget had taught them that, as a rule, humans tended to ignore the unusual because it was easier to believe what fit neatly into their worldview.

Crime-fighting rodents did not fit into most people's worldview.

This was an advantage for every Watcher.

The Mouse Watch always tried to hide its activities from human eyes as much as possible, and this human tendency toward denial worked to their benefit. It helped them to get from place to place in public while avoiding detection.

As Bernie and her best friend sped to their target, hoping beyond hope that they wouldn't be too late, she wondered what the mission would be. They hadn't been told exactly *who* they were rescuing or from *what*, but it had to be important if they'd been directed to drop everything to get there so quickly.

To calm her nerves as she raced along, she recited the Mouse Watch creed to herself:

Every part of a watch is important, from the smallest gear on up. For without each part working together, keeping time is impossible. We never sleep. We never fail. We are there for all who call upon us in their time of need. We are the MOUSE WATCH!

And with the inspirational thought of those very special words, words that meant everything to her, Bernie took courage and raced on into the gathering darkness, anxious to get to their destination before time ran out.